PENGUIN

WILLIAM M

The Truth at Last

Spike Milligan was born in Ahmednagar in India in 1919, received his first education in a tent in the Hyderabad Sindh desert and graduated from there through a series of Roman Catholic Schools in India and England to the Lewisham Polytechnic. Always something of a playboy, he then plunged into the world of show business, seduced by his first stage appearance, at the age of eight, in the nativity play of his Poona convent school. He began his career as a band musician but has since become famous as a humorous scriptwriter and actor both in films and broadcasting, in particular, the infamous Goon Show. Spike Milligan's books in Penguins are *Puckoon*, *Small Dreams of a Scorpion*, *Transports of Delight* and his war trilogy, *Adolf Hitler: My Part in His Downfall*, *'Rommel: Gunner Who?'* and *Monty: His Part in My Victory*. His latest publication is *The Spike Milligan Letters*, edited by Norma Farnes. Spike Milligan is married, has three children and lives in London.

Jack Hobbs was born in Bradford in 1926. He served in the Army until 1947 and stayed as a civilian working and travelling about until 1950 when he returned to England and became a bookseller. In 1958 he started, with John Rolph, the Scorpion Press, publishing poetry. In 1966 he started M&J Hobbs Publishers specializing in humour, and has since published fourteen books by Spike Milligan and other titles by Harry Secombe, Johnny Speight, Ronnie Corbett, Bill Tidy and others. He has co-written three books with Spike Milligan and is also the author of *Cats in Verse*. Recently he wrote a comedy for television with John Cleese and Joe McGrath. When he has time he paints and plays jazz piano. He is married, has three sons and hides in Walton-on-Thames.

AUL B., MORGAN

William McGonagall

The Truth at Last

Shock Horror - a fantasia by
SPIKE MILLIGAN
& JACK HOBBS

illustrated by
ANYBODY & PETER SELLERS

PENGUIN BOOKS

Penguin Books Ltd, Harmondsworth, Middlesex, England
Penguin Books, 625 Madison Avenue, New York, New York 10022, U.S.A.
Penguin Books Australia Ltd, Ringwood, Victoria, Australia
Penguin Books Canada Ltd, 2801 John Street, Markham, Ontario, L3R 1B4 Canada
Penguin Books (N.Z.) Ltd, 182–190 Wairau Road, Auckland 10, New Zealand

—

First published by M & J Hobbs and Michael Joseph Ltd 1976
Published in Penguin Books 1978

—

Copyright © Spike Milligan Productions Ltd and Jack Hobbs, 1976
All rights reserved

—

Made and printed in Great Britain
by Richard Clay (The Chaucer Press) Ltd
Bungay, Suffolk
Set in Linotype Baskerville

Except in the United States of America,
this book is sold subject to the condition
that it shall not, by way of trade or otherwise,
be lent, re-sold, hired out, or otherwise circulated
without the publisher's prior consent in any form of
binding or cover other than that in which it is
published and without a similar condition
including this condition being imposed
on the subsequent purchaser

W. McGonagall was born in 1843/44/45.
You see there was a great degree of uncertainty in the family and they called it William McGonagall by which time he was 6.30 on Platform 9.

A BRIEF BIOGRAPHY

BORN: 1843/4/5
HIT: 1856/7/8/9
DIED: 1900
BURIED: 1936/7/8

SMALL BROTHER
FUEL
McGONIGAL

McGONICALS
FATHER

MOTHER
VERA
SMITH-
-JONES
-BROWN.
FROM A DIFFERENT
STORY

SISTER
HATTIE.

P. SELLES

War broke out in 1939 – when he rejoined the colours – red, green, orange and mauve which later became the County of Westmorland, where he was born the following year 1843/4/5.

MARLBERG McGONICALLOCKS
ANCESTOR 1588.

SPERM McGONAGAL

COUSIN
SHIT
McGONAGALL

CHAPTER I

To the devotee, William McGonagall died in Edinburgh on the 29th September 1902. The reaction to this in South Africa was the outbreak of the Boer War which is borne out by the document from Fred Rollo – from Zululand – which died with him alas. A spokesman for the Times Literary Supplement said, 'I am a spokesman for the Times Lit. Supp. and I now go on to say – William McGonagall is a real genius for he is the only memorable truly bad poet in our language.'

Having read this comment in the Acton Steelworkers Monthly, (an offshoot of the Times), William McGonagall dashed off an immortal brief poem. Which was, '**** the spokesman for the Times Literary Supplement!'

The costly litigation which followed this bankrupted him. In the final summing up, Judge Arlington Balls said:

'William McGonagall would you repeat for this court exactly the poem.'

'Yes, my Lord.' (Laughter in court)

'A poem to the Spokesman of the Times Literary Supplement by William T. McGonagall. Oooooooooooooo-ohhhhhhhhhh **** the spokesman of the Times Literary Supplement. Ooooooooooooooo.'

JUDGE: 'Six months and costs.'

McG: 'Ooooooooooooooooooohhhhhhhhhhhh ****!'

9

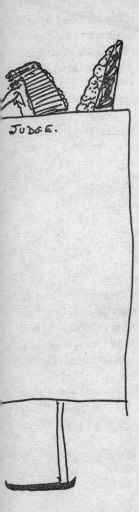

JUDGE.

P. Sellas

As McGonagall was led down the stairs he tried to sell his suit to the constable saying 'You can have it mounted, and stuffed after my death, and it will be worth a fortune.' Whereupon the constable had to be restrained from strangling him on the spot. The cruel sentence only generated the muse even more. In his filthy cell in Newgate prison he wrote : —

> 'Oooooooooooooooohhhh what a terrible thing
> it is to be in gaol,
> But I'll soon be out without fail,
> The moment my sentence is up,
> I will leave here to go out and eat and sup,
> And that foolish judge Arlington Balls
> Will be forced to pay to see me
> When I am on the Music Halls.
> And when I see him sitting in the front row
> I will say "Hello you merry fellow —
> Ying tong iddle I po".'

During his stay in prison he lost weight and he had to force feed himself to keep up his strength. About this time a second inmate was hurled into his cell who turned out to be a young Hindu by the name of Ghandi, a political agitator and baritone sax player in the all-Hindu Kush Band, but nobody believed him.

They struck up a great friendship. In a cell three foot by eight there was nothing much else they could do. They tried hitting each other but it didn't work out. McGonagall wrote a great limerick which went,

> There was a young man called Ghandi
> Who went in the bar for a shandy.
> With his great loincloth
> He wiped off the froth
> And the barman said, 'Blimey that's 'andy.'

Ghandi never knuckled down to prison conditions. Every time he heard the keys jangling in the cell door he said : 'Quick the police — under the bed.'

McGonagall planned an escape which went like this.

'One day I'm going to get out of here.'

He struck on a master plan. During the next three months from the bedposts he whittled a wooden leg. From Ghandi's jockstrap he made an eyepatch. From the cardboard in the window he made a tricorn hat. By using wire from the bedsprings he strapped one leg up his back and inverting a broom under his arm like a crutch he struck a dinnertime pose, while Ghandi shouted through the grill 'There's a man sick in here.' When the Gaoler arrived, McGonagall said, 'You've sentenced the wrong man. I am Long John Silver.' Next day he appeared in court and was given three years for piracy.

'Thank you, your honour,' he said. 'It's better than the last sentence.'

McGONAGALL AND GHANDI IN PRISON

In the ensuing fight, the leg fell off and was loudly applauded by the Jury.

When the eyepatch fell off, followed by the tricorn hat, he cried, 'Hold, I am not Long John Silver, but the Poet/ Impressionist William McGonagall.'

He was put on bread and water in solitary for fourteen days for a breach of the peace, and it made a nice change from Ghandi who, without the controlling influence of a jockstrap, had become politically agitated.

Whilst in solitary with twenty other men he wrote the following tender poem.

McGONAGALL
AND FELLOW
PRISONERS

Ooooooooooooooooooooooooooooooooooo
ooooooooooooooooooooooooooooooooo
ooooooooooooooooooooooooooooo
oooooooooooooooooooooooooooooohhhh
I am in solitary with twenty other men
And I don't want to do it again,
Whereas usually in the dark I have no fears
But some naughty convict was twisting my ears.
And I would say 'Stop that Tommy or Dick or
  Jim'
Or whichever of those names belonged to him.
For there's nothing so unfunny as a mistake in
  the dark.
With some naughty convict who thinks it's a lark.
And there some things they did I don't
  understand
Like some terrible thing they put in my hand.

P. Soras

Six months to the day he was discharged from Newgate clutching a sheaf of poems, a blanket and Ghandi's jock-strap, a farewell gift from his Hindu friend.

At about this time fortune smiled on him but did nothing else. The distance between Scotland and London is some 400 miles, but he did it in some 632 miles. 'I'll get it right next time,' he was heard to say.

'Ooooooh the distance between London and Scotland
  is hard to bear.
To say it is 400 miles is hardly fair
When I did it it was 632
But then I was following an old wandering Jew
Who was looking for the promised land
Which unfortunately was not to hand.
'Is this the promised land?' he said of Dundee,
'Aye,' I said, 'But it's been promised to me.'
He then struck me with his Jewish nose,
So I threw him in the river and burnt all his clothes.
Because no man is going to get the better of me,
At least not within the sight of the city of Dundee.
For I have nice relatives staying there,
And to see me burning Jewish clothes would not be
  fair.

So McGonagall continued on his merry way, his shoes now grievously in need of repair, as were his feet. They were so worn that he was hospitalized at the Scottish Malt Whiskey Hospital. A doctor asked him what was the matter.

'It's my feet,' he said.
'How many miles have they done?' asked the doctor.
'632 Jewish miles,' replied McGonagall.
'I'll soon have them back to their own cheery self,' said the doctor.

That night he was operated on. When he regained

consciousness his first words were 'My feet don't feel any better and I mean that most sincerely.'

The doctor said, 'We didnae touch your feet, we played safe – we operated on you for piles,' to which McGonagall smilingly replied, 'But I hannae gae any.'

'Och well,' said the doctor, putting on a Scottish accent, 'You gae em the noo.'

From his window he could see first his feet, and beyond into the bonny Sidlaw Hills and he penned a verse to the night sister, Bonny Clara, or Pisspot Annie as she was affectionately known to the Indian Lascars who played her at dominoes in the Hairy Bells Public Hoose.

She was 6ft 3in and smothered in red hair, McGonagall fell madly in love with her and wrote this tender verse:

> Bonny Clara will ye go to the bonny Sidlaw Hills
> And pu' the blooming heather and drink from
> their rills
> There the cranberries among the heather grow
> Believe me, dear Clara, as black as the crow.

Translated into seaman's jargon:

> Bonny Pisspot Annie lying stoned on the hills
> The last chap that was with you lost both of his
> pills
> And they lie among the cranberries making the
> heather grow
> Believe me Pisspot Annie you haven't got long
> to go.

To commemorate the tenth anniversary of the battle of Trafalgar, William McGonagall was discharged from the hospital, and his bed burnt and sold to the V. & A. Museum who had mistaken it for an early, (about 6.30 a.m.), Kurdish shepherd's wind harp for soothing sheep during attacks of rabies – and by a strange quirk of fate that's exactly what it turned out to be. No wonder McGonagall had never slept well and left hospital with rabies.

17

PURE 100 PROOF ROTTEN
MALT WHISKEY

Poverty finally forced him to return to his mother and father's home in Dundee, where in fact they had been forced by poverty. His mother was delighted to see him. His father split his head open with a loaded sock. Fourteen stitches later McGonagall repaired to his little room which his mother had carefully kept exactly how he had left it – filthy.

Owing to lack of unemployment McGonagall was forced to take work at ex-provost Reid's factory which was turning out underwear for the troops fighting the Boers in South Africa. McGonagall mastered the art of handlooming. He did this by waiting for dark nights in dark alleys then painting his hands with phosphorescent

paint which made his hands loom out of the darkness. It
was a strange way to make a living but then so was
Pisspot Annie. At this time he wrote his 'Ode to a Hand-
loomer.'

OOOOOoooooooooohhhh –

Oh beautiful handlooming factory of
   Scouringburn,
   The place I attended for to learn
How to make hands loom,
To produce an export boom,
And I must thank the owner,
   Mr Peter Davie,
Who had absolutely nothing to do with
Her Majesty's Brittanic Navy.

He showed this poem to Mr Davie and it did not take
him very long to get another job. He became gainfully
employed as a human bullet in Doctor Chicago's Lion
Circus. It was a very simple job. He was, twice a night,
strapped to a stretcher and loaded into a cannon. He
was billed as the singing bullet, for it was his task to

burst into song as he was fired out to sea. His world record was one and a half choruses of Ave Maria from point of exit to point of entry.

He was never the same after this, but then he had never been the same before, and the effect of repeated immersion in the English Channel during the month of December was having a grievous effect upon his health – he was drowning. He decided to fight back by using the word 'HELP' whenever he surfaced. He was saved by a Scottish dentist who was walking his toothless dog along the cliffs when he heard the word 'HELP.' The dentist yelled 'Try Miaouw.' Being in no position to argue, McGonagall complied. 'Miaouw' he went, whereupon he was immediately attacked in the water by a toothless dog, which pulled him ashore and savaged him with its gums.

'You're a lucky man,' said the dentist. 'I hid his teeth this morning. I had a feeling something like this would happen – Have you ever heard of Scott Fitzgerald?'

'No,' said McGonagall.

'Thank God, then – he's safe,' said the Scottish dentist. The dentist asked McGonagall to roll up his trouser legs.

'It's a strange request,' said McGonagall, 'but as you have just saved my life and my legs are part of that, I'll do so.' He rolled his trousers up as far as the knee whereupon the dentist, slipping the dog's teeth back into it, shouted, 'Here Rover – dinner's ready.' McGonagall carried the marks for the rest of his life and the dog died of rabies.

Later that day.

An elderly lady sitting in her front room knitting ammunition for our brave boys in South Africa, while her husband was eating food for the brave lads at the front in South Africa, beheld a strange sight. Slowly moving through the heather came a Scotsman, with his trouser legs rolled up, teeth marks on his legs, and all the while reciting poetry. Stranger still, it wasn't McGonagall. It was the Scott FitzGerald. He cried out to the lady,

'Have you ever heard of William Gonagall?'

'No,' said the old lady.

His reply was drowned out by the roar of an exploding woollen grenade that had detonated, deafening the old lady for life, but it was assumed by the lip-reading husband that the Scott FitzGerald had said 'The lang kilt o' the Laird McToole cannae cover his Kung Fu.' It was a lie of course but then nobody lived to tell the tale because at that moment the dinner exploded killing the husband, his deaf wife, and the Scott FitzGerald in the record time of 1 minute 30 seconds.

CHAPTER II

With the three main characters dead we are forced to return to McGonagall who we find in a Scottish Leg Hospital in charge of the Poison Cupboard. The job didn't last long nor did anybody else in the hospital. At the mass funeral he wasn't present, but he left a note saying 'I'm sorry.' together with this poem: –

The Terrible Poisoning of all the Inmates of the Scottish Leg Hospital

Oooooooohhhh in the year 1892
When most oft the Highland Hairies were
    stricken doon with floo,
At which time William McGonagall of whom it
    was said,
'He is working in the Scottish Leg Hospital
    counting the dead'
Had taken charge of the poisons there,
And by the time he had finished the poison
    cupboard was bare.
And all around him the patients were groaning
    and going 'Oh'
And by the look of some of them they didn't
    have very long to go.
For William McGonagall would not take the
    blame oh no, not a bit,
For he didn't know the difference between
    arsenic and manure.

There were bottles of arsenic on every shelf,
And McGonagall let each of the patients help
  himself.
Some of the silly patients put poison in their
  soup,
And the pain was so intense some of them did
  the loop.
And McGonagall stood there filled with despair,
  it's sad to relate,
Within minutes three inside the Scottish Leg
  Hospital he was the only surviving inmate.
Save for one last victim, he thought to be dead,
  who rose up from his coffin and threw a brick
  at his head.
And soon a coroner to the spot did arrive,
And said, 'Oh deary me, there's no-one left
  alive.'
'What about me,' said McGonagall as on the
  table he did mount.
But the coroner, looking quite surprised, said
  'Freaks like you don't count.'

This latest tragedy did for McGonagall but not as much as it did for the inmates. The empty hospital lay still and silent – open to the elements. At night all you would hear was the mournful wind whistling up the chimneys, the skeletal rattle of the windows' shutters, and the merry whistling of William McGonagall as he painted a 'For Sale' sign. But the loneliness of the place became unbearable. He packed up his brief belongings and left the Scottish Leg Hospital to its ghosts.

The great driving force that was known as William McGonagall was now to become infatuated with the world of acting. He wished to purchase a complete set of Shakespeare's Penny Plays, but was waiting for them to fall in price. He finally obtained a complete set from a Chinese ventriloquist who had no right to have them. The terms

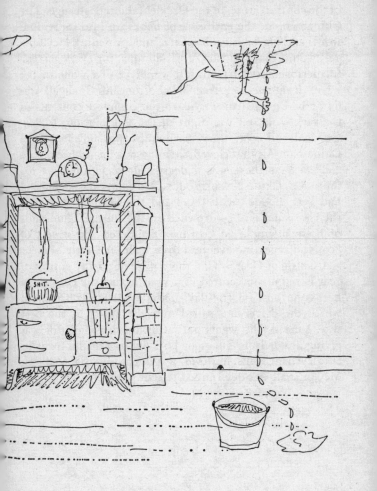

of the contract were, to the Occidental mind, strange. The Chinaman cut the entire set of books up into individual words and placed them in a sack, and, providing McGonagall would play the part of his dummy, for every successful performance McGonagall would be given one of the words from the sack free. By the time McGonagall was 63 he had gained the rights to the complete contents of the sack. Alas, on the night of the termination, to McGonagall's horror, the ventriloquist was not in fact a Chinaman. All that clever scheming was for nothing.

That year there was a dearth of unemployment for imitation Chinese ventriloquist's dummies, the market had been flooded with them and the hillside rang with their screams as they drowned in the burns. Thousands of these unemployed creatures wandered the streets of Scotland repeating over and over again 'A Gottle of Gear – A Gottle of Gear' – alas, there were not many gottles of gear being manufactured that year, in fact the gear trade had gone bust on the day of the Wall Street Crash in which the driver was killed outright, which is the best way. I mean who wants partial death? None of this was giving any help to our poor boys fighting at the front in South Africa. This, however, was something that William McGonagall was determined to stamp out.

CHAPTER III

On the SS *Phillys* he booked a third class ticket to Durban. It was a fine craft with a slight tendency to sink. The captain reassured the passengers, 'Och aye,' which was a funny start for a Frenchman. 'Zis leetle sheep iss unsinkable.' 'Why then,' thought McGonagall, 'did the crew, every night, sleep in the lifeboats?' The captain gave a word of warning. 'I advise all passengers to give their valuables and moneys to me for the safekeeping on the voyage.' Three days after that no sight of the captain had been seen. Cautiously McGonagall asked the purser if his money was safe with the captain. 'Of course,' said the purser, 'perfectly safe, wherever he and his motor launch are.' 'Are you implying,' said McGonagall, 'that my money has been stolen?' 'No,' said the purser, 'consider it more as a floating loan,' he said, and added, 'Wherever he and his motor launch are.'

McGonagall never recovered from this blow though why the purser hit him he was at a loss to imagine. On landing at Durban he was immediately classified as a nigger and was sent up the line as a second class kaffir, humping ammunition. He bore all this very stoically and again the muse flowered.

> Ooooo when I reached that golden city of
>   Durban
> To stop getting sun stroke I tried on a turban.

As I wound it on my head it got bigger and
     bigger
And a kind voice behind said 'That man's a
     nigger.'
Glad to be accepted as a native of the land
I grinned at him merrily and held out my hand,
And thereupon without further delay
They threw me on a bullock cart and took me
     away.
We drove through scenery both beautiful and
     grand
As they shovelled in all kinds of rocks and sand
For the journey I was making up to the front –

The last line evaded the poet as he came under heavy
shellfire from the Boers and later on, after only three readings, from the British.

McGonagall was now in the heart of historic Zululand
which wasn't doing it any good. His special command
performance appearance, dressed as Macbeth, before the
Zulu chief Dingaan, had him clubbed to the ground. He
was only saved from having the traditional stake ham-
mered up his rectum by Mrs. Hazel Grollecks who just
happened to be in the right place at the right time. She
had a soothing effect upon Dingaan, which consisted of
The Siberian Sexual Head Massage which cured bed-
wetting and piles. As he walked from the Kraal, bloody
but unhurt, he turned to her and said, 'I don't know who
you are ma'am, I dinnae ken where you're frae, but ye've
done me a power of gude.' Which in fact was true, but she
was doing the king much better. He was getting it three
times a night and it had reduced the swelling consider-
ably. Up front the battle for the Tugg eliah Cobblers was
at its height, when McGonagall wrote home to his family.

'Dear Mother and Father,

I am in South Africa on holiday. The weather is really
beautiful here. They tell me a war has broken out which

28

AS MACBETH

makes travelling difficult, but I seem to be well liked everywhere I go. The only trouble is I don't go anywhere. I was personally clubbed to the ground by the Zulu King which they tell me is a great honour. I was dressed as Macbeth at the time in a costume made from ex-army blankets, which must have helped.

At the present moment I have not many engagements apart from dysentry.

I am preparing to give performances at the front to both sides during lulls in the shelling. For safety I do this from a hole in the ground which I excavate the night before. To let them know where I am, I hold up a card-board replica of myself and shout the lines loudly in both directions.

Unfortunately so far, these performances have been marred by an intensification of firing by both sides at my trench. I think it is, in their rough soldierly manner, their way of saying thank you.

Please send more pile ointment and a fresh sock. I am returning the other one under separate cover for launder-ing. Please tell them not to starch it so much this time as it is making me walk with a limp.

> Your loving son,
> William.

P.S. Up South Africa.'

Indeed the P.S. gave an irrevocable clue to the suffer-ing he was undergoing. During the performance of Hamlet from a tree overlooking the Boer trenches, he contracted sunstroke which coincided with the felling of the tree by Boer Engineers. When he regained conscious-ness he lay in a shallow grave which was being filled in.

'Goddemmitt men! He's come to. Get him out and put him on a stretcher!' He was put on a stretcher and stretched to six foot three inches, when rain stopped play and shrinkage took place, restoring him to his vital self.

Along with Winston Churchill he escaped from the Boer's compound. When Churchill heard this he climbed back in. He made his way back to the British lines just in time for the battle of Rouark's Drift. Of this battle he wrote.

> Oooooooooohhh brave Dublin Fusiliers
> Who went to the front filled with fears,
> For that night they were to fight for
>   Rouark's Drift
> And they stood by the wayside
>   thumbing a lift,
> For all of their transport had been set on fire
> By a drunken comrade called Fusilier McGuire,
> And as the flames from the conflagration
>   grew higher
> It made some of the spectators for to perspire.
>
> Meanwhile around them the Boers were
>   dropping shells,
> And those that were hit were heard to give off
>   loud yells.
> And Captain O'Brien who was hit in the knee
> Said 'Hurry up boys or we'll miss our tea.'
> And the brave fusiliers, they put on a spurt
> And Sergeant Ryan fell dead with a bullet
>   through his shirt,
> Whereupon the Fusiliers all did fix bayonets
> And the Boers were heard to shout
>   'That's enough, we give up, feynits.'
> Thus was the battle of Rouark's Drift won.
> It was far from easy and not much fun.

One morning while serving tea to General Roberts, he woke him up with the following: 'The best laid plans of mice and men oft gang aglae.' Roberts sat up and said, 'Do you like Burns?' McGonagall nodded, whereupon General Roberts stuck a red-hot poker up his nose.

McGonagall reeled backwards, reeled forwards and

then reeled upright – but then Scotland was always famous for its reels. By mutual agreement, between the Boers and the British it was agreed that both sides would fire upon him whenever he appeared. He sought refuge by blacking himself up but alas was immediately con-scripted into a Kaffir regiment. He gave himself away when the sergeant said 'Eyes right.' McGonagall replied, 'No you'se wrong. *I'se* right.' They shot him – he never recovered – and remained dead for the rest of his life.

On leave from the Kaffir regiment he journeyed to Cape Town where a Jewish cameraman persuaded him to pose for accidents, as there was a shortage of victims. He front-paged for a week with the Rand Daily Mail in such headlines as 'COLOURED SCOTSMAN RUN DOWN BY STEAM ROLLER,' next day, 'COLOURED SCOTSMAN RENDERED UNCONSCIOUS BY TRAIN.' After a week of accidents, clutching a pay cheque for £3 12s and paralysed, he was hospitalized again in the famous NIGGER LEG HOSPITAL at Cape Town where he entertained Kaffirs with merry Scots songs, Othello excerpts, and readings of his poem

> Ooo-o-ooh 'twas on the 3rd April 1902
> When a Kaffir wearing the uniform of a
>   soldier blue
> Was on leave in the beautiful village of Cape
>   Town
> Where he did walk up the streets and then
>   sometimes walked down.
> He was on leave from one of the Colonial wars,
> And this one was between the British and the
>   Boers,
> And the battle all year had been raging,
> And amongst the many troops there were indeed
>   some sign of ageing.
> But McGonagall had stepped onto the field and
>   said 'Stop the battle's tide!'

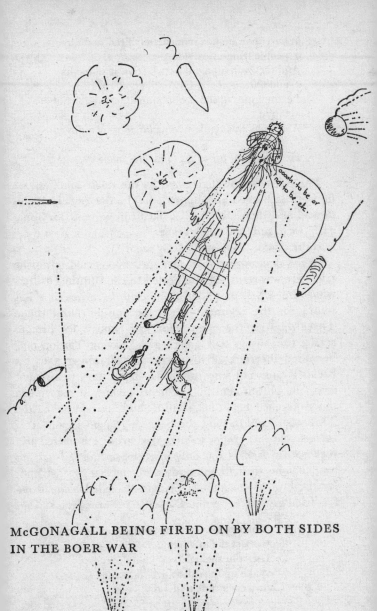

McGONAGALL BEING FIRED ON BY BOTH SIDES
IN THE BOER WAR

Whereupon he was immediately fired upon by
  people from every side
And the bullets passed between his legs, teeth
  and hair.
Leading him to shout out 'Stop all this – it's not
  fair.'
And as he was rendered unconscious by a direct
  hit,
He was heard for to say 'This has made me unfit.'

The poem was well received by the Kaffir inmates and
he was discharged and upgraded. The doctor said 'Bend
down,' and then said 'C3.' 'That's funny,' said McGonagall. 'I can only see two.' 'Have you ever had a glass eye?'
said the doctor. 'No,' said McGonagall.

So the doctor gave him one, and this seemed to do the
trick. He was returned and posted to the Dublin Fusiliers
where he was kept under a stone, until a position was
found for the regiment where he couldn't find them.
Three days on the open veldt was enough for him to
realize that things had 'gang a-glae.' Saying 'Pardon me,'
he rolled the rock off his chest, and strapping it to his
back, 'I must not lose this piece of military equipment
from the Dublin Fusiliers. For all I know it may mean
the difference between winning and losing the battle.
This stone could swing the balance.' So he set off at as
brisk a pace as could be managed with a hundred ton
rock on his back. It was only when he saw a snail passing
him that he realized the odds were stacked against him.
By the end of the month he had travelled some three
feet from his starting point. Deep inside a voice was saying,

'Don't you know little fool
you never can win.
Use your mentality
Wake up to reality.'
And each time that I do

34

Just the thought of you
Makes me stop before I begin
'Cos I've got you under my skin –
and this is Cole Porter saying it.

An ambulance passed him carrying the dead. 'Get in,' said the driver, 'before it's too late.' 'Are you Cole Porter?' said McGonagall. 'No,' said the driver, 'I'm Fusilier Scott Fitzgerald.'

Sitting on the back of a pile of dead Boers, he observed that there was also a pile of English dead bores but he couldn't tell the difference because of the spelling. He sang a merry song from amid the bodies, a thing he did remarkably well. The driver was heard to say 'Have you been trained for this sort of thing?' 'No,' said McGonagall. 'It just comes naturally.' 'Have you ever raised the dead?' said the driver, 'No,' said McGonagall. 'Well you have now,' said the driver, 'The bloody wagon's empty.'

McGONAGALL CARRYING A 100 TON ROCK FOR NO REASON AT ALL

'I never knew I could exercise such power,' said McGonagall, 'I must try it again, can we go back for another load?'

'I'm sorry,' said the driver, 'It's early closing back there, but I think there's a much better war going on in Abyssinia where there is a good selection of stiffs.' 'Oh no,' said McGonagall, 'I would travel far to raise the dead again but I may not be able to raise Abyssinians. It would be a bitter disappointment to me if they did not react favourably, for after all I will be speaking English and they may not understand.' And he burst into tears. 'Is it something I've said?' said the driver. 'No, it's this 100 ton rock on my back,' said McGonagall. 'The ropes are cutting into my powerful chest.' 'Have you ever thought of carrying a lighter one?' said the driver. 'Yes,' said McGonagall, 'but it didn't help. And in any case to carry a lighter rock would mean a change of regiment. I know for a fact that the Ox & Bucks Light Infantry only carry 40 lb rocks on their backs, but then they march quicker than the Dublin Fusiliers. They get to the battlefields earlier, and get killed more quickly and who wants that? I'm not such an idiot as I look.' 'Funny you should say that,' said the driver. 'Why?' said McGonagall. 'Nothing, it's just funny that you should say that.' 'That's alright then,' said McGonagall. 'Just so long as I know.'

The cart drove on in silence save for the odd noises that horses are wont to make. 'That's a fine horse you've got,' said McGonagall. 'I would say that he was about three years old.' 'My father used to be –' 'Used to be what?' said McGonagall. 'I don't know,' said the driver. 'I never got as far as that. And my mother,' went on the driver, 'always wore a large black dress to offset her teeth, and they set off quite often in fact. They were once found wandering in Highgate Cemetery.' McGonagall rolled a fresh pipe of tobacco and said 'A horse is a friend for life.' 'And on summers nights my father used to apply leeches

36

to my mother's head – it seemed a good idea at the time but now with the high price of leeches, she has to go without.'

'I would never hit a horse myself,' said McGonagall, 'unless he struck me first,' and lit the pipe. A wisp of smoke escaped from the bowl of his pipe. He immediately inserted a fresh wisp. 'You would think,' said the driver, 'with Borneo full of leeches that the price would have come down, but no, there was my mother walking round with an un-leeched head.'

'One horse at a time is enough,' said McGonagall, 'after that things become complicated – I mean if there's *one*, that's alright, but if there's *three* you have to add them up every night to see if they're all there. I mean you can always see when one horse is all there.'

'That goes for leeches,' said the driver. 'That was the trouble in the first place. You see, the leeches slipped away one by one and she never noticed. If there had only been one leech we would have noticed if it had gone. Of course a single leech can slip away in the dark, but this one didn't. It slipped away during the day.'

Suddenly McGonagall burst into a song:

> Ooooooooooh dreaded leeches stuck on the
>   head,
> They'll only stay there as long as they're fed.
> And so a Scottish death cart driver did say
> 'They wait until the dark and then they slip
>   away.'
> But that could never happen with a noble
>   horse
> They always stand where they are of course.
> If only the husband had instead
> Placed horses on his beloved wife's head,
> Then she could have walked through the
>   market place
> With people saying to her 'You're no
>   disgrace.'

And now that poor Scottish wife's head is
   a terrible scene
You cannot see leeches but you can see
   where they've been.

They drove in a silence broken only by the sickening thud of the driver's fist on McGonagall's throat. 'I've never liked poetry,' said the driver, 'and I've never liked leeches, and I never liked my mother's head. To find all three in the same poem is bad casting. I would like to have used Sir Henry Irving, Marie Lloyd and Little Tich, but now it's too late for that,' and continued to thud McGonagall's throat.

McGonagall was very glad when he stopped it. The journey seemed woefully slow. 'If we both got off this cart it would go much quicker,' said McGonagall. 'You're right,' said the driver, and they both dismounted, and away went the wagon at a much brisker pace. The silence was broken only by the thudding of the driver's fist on McGonagall's throat. 'Stop it,' said McGonagall. 'I'm not reciting poetry.' 'This is not reciting-poetry-thudding,' said the driver. 'This is "getting-off-the-cart-so's-we-can-go-quicker - and - having - eight - days - shagged - out - walking - through-the-bush" type thudding.' 'Thank God for that,' said McGonagall. 'There is a marked difference, and most of the marks are on me.'

'No hard feelings?' said the driver. 'No,' said McGonagall, 'just lumps.' 'I'm sorry I'm acting like this,' said the driver, 'but I've never been in a Boer War before and it's thrown me completely.'

'It didn't throw you far enough,' said McGonagall.

'I'm really a Crimea man you know,' said the driver, 'when that stopped I suffered withdrawal symptoms.'

'Withdrawal symptoms?' queried McGonagall.

'Yes, I was in the middle of having it off with this Russian woman, when this bloke said "The war's over," and pulled me off.'

'*He* pulled you off?' said McGonagall.

'Yes,' said the driver.

'Oh,' said McGonagall.

'P' said the driver.

'Q' said McGonagall,

and so they went hand in hand through the alphabet and only stopped once for 'T'. It was a hot afternoon and very educational.

'Look at this newspaper,' said McGonagall. 'BOER WAR OVER.'

'Oh God,' said the driver, 'what am I going to do now?'

'Look for your cart,' said McGonagall.

They agreed at this moment to go their different ways, McGonagall with a cheery wave of his hand, the driver with a smiling thud to the throat.

Diary entry of a patient in the Boer Throat Hospital in Natal:

'Have not spoken a word for two months . . .'

The next day

'I have not spoken a word for two months and a day' – a great pity as there are poems raging through my head awaiting for my fiery pen to commit them to paper, but I will never know what they are until I hear them spoken. Why, oh why did that terrible driver thud my noble throat, and why, oh why was I there when he did it? If only I'd stayed away, his blows would have landed on thin air.'

McGonagall received daily visits from a mortician who insisted on asking him how he felt. McGonagall wrote on a piece of paper 'I'm alright.' The mortician immediately burned it and wrote, 'I know that but which way are you going – my advice is buy now while wood is cheap?,' and measured McGonagall. McGonagall wrote, 'I'll think about it.'

That night the night sister found the mortician under the bed doing sums on the back of his shovel. 'Is this man a friend of yours?' she said. McGonagall nodded and wrote: 'Aye and he's promised me a Christmas box.' But the night sister gave McGonagall a long penetrating look, noting his red-rimmed eyes, and the hairs on the palm of his hand, and said, 'You'll go blind if you don't stop it.'

Wrote McGonagall, 'I have nae slept a wink since I came here.' 'You see it's keeping you awake as well,' she said. 'No,' he wrote, 'I think it's this 100 ton rock on my back.' 'Rock?' she said. 'We've been treating you as a hunchback – you should have said.' 'But I can't speak,' he wrote. With a quick flash of her scissors she cut the ropes and removed the stone. 'I'll have to show this to the doctor, it could be the cause of the trouble,' said the sister, 'He specializes in stones in the kidney and he'll want to know why it wasn't there, so you'd better have a good excuse ready.'

In one bound she was gone, and with another bound she was back again. 'Have your bowels moved today?' she said. 'No,' he wrote, 'they've been with me all the time.' In one bound McGonagall was gone. 'I've had enough of this place,' he said. Next morning the mortician buried an empty bed. It had been a lesson to all three of them, and in one bound all three were gone.

Using his superb knowledge of contortionism, that night McGonagall slept by the wayside in a rucksack, for which he was charged £22. 10s, by a man dressed as a hotel manager. 'Is this a hotel?' said McGonagall. 'No, but it will be,' said the man, 'as soon as the walls are up. It's open plan you understand.' 'I want to be called at 7.30 in the morning,' said McGonagall. Sure enough at 7.30 in the morning a man came and called him an idiot.

He spent three uncomfortable but expensive nights at this wayside Hilton, and with a superb sense of orientation realized he was sleeping along the grid line of 190 degrees N. by N.E.; that is, if you drew a line down his body across Africa and continued it through into Lewisham, it would pass directly through the centre of Mrs Mountain's Dining Rooms for Gentlemen of the Transport Industry, and McGonagall remembered many fine dinners there. In particular he remembered the great meal on Burns Night known as The Mrs Mountain Burnt Meals on Wheels Speciality.

He then penned the following ode to Mrs Mountain's Dining Rooms: –

> Oooooooooooooh Mrs Mountain's fine and
>   wonderful Transport Cafe,
> For which many men have shouted hip hip
>   hooray
> And the nights there were always cheerful and
>   good
> And I would go there again if it were not for the
>   terrible food.
> The reason for its popularity is that the prices
>   are very cheap,
> But the food is thrown at you in a bloody great
>   heap.
> And sometimes it misses and goes crashing to
>   the floor
> Where it is eaten by people who live under
>   tables and are said to be very poor.
> But still Scottish and Jewish diners come to
>   eat from afar
> Despite the fact that when they do not pay she
>   splits their heads open with an iron bar.
> McGonagall remembers when he was hurled
>   through the window under a passing lorry,
> And because he had not paid he was heard for
>   to shout 'I'm sorry.'

He stayed in bed reminiscing, which cost him extra. 'Where now?' thought McGonagall as he donned his morning clothes. Climbing down the knotted sheets he met someone coming the other way. It was the manager. 'We've heard of you,' he said. 'This will cost you extra.' 'I haven't any more money,' said McGonagall. 'That's the wrong answer,' said the manager. 'I tell you what, I can get you a job on board my brother's slave ship.'

CHAPTER IV

That night, under a full moon, McGonagall sailed from South Africa, in the hold, as a slave. 'I want to see my solicitor,' he shouted through the barred hatch. 'Keep rowing or you'll have us all on the rocks,' shouted a friendly voice.

> It was the captain of the lugger
> Known as Captain Dan MacGrugger
> He wasn't fit
> . . .

And that was why McGonagall was rowing. 'What's the name of this ship?' said McGonagall. 'The Marie Celeste,' came the reply.

'I've got a nasty feeling,' said McGonagall.

'Well, keep it to yourself,' said the Captain, 'and I'll tell you what we'll do, we'll split the insurance.'

They spent the rest of the day pushing the crew overboard and setting the table for breakfast.

'Just before we lower the lifeboat,' said the Captain, 'put two sausages, bacon and eggs on every plate – That'll fool 'em.'

'It fooled me,' said McGonagall. But then everything did. As they rowed from the silent, fully rigged ship, the Captain gloated over the side. 'Oh wait till we collect the insurance on that,' he said, 'it'll come to a tidy sum.' 'How much is that?' said McGonagall. 'Five pounds each,' said the Captain. 'That's not much for the loss of a big ship like that,' said McGonagall. 'My God you're right,' said the Captain. 'Quick, after it.'

But row as he might McGonagall couldn't catch the fast disappearing *Marie Celeste*. 'She must be making all of twenty-three knots,' said the Captain. 'Oh dear,' said McGonagall. 'I only know how to make two, and one of those is a granny.' Try as he may, they could not close the gap. With McGonagall at the oars the Captain rowed like mad, but steer as he may he had no effect.

Log of the lifeboat 321:

DAY ONE – Enough food and water to last us for three months.

DAY TWO – All food and water gone.

DAY THREE – Dying of thirst and hunger.

DAY FOUR – McGonagall lying delirious in the scuppers saying to himself 'Oooooooooooh Mrs Mountain's glorious Transport Cafe, where are ye in my hour of need?,' to which she replied, 'I'm here in Lewisham cooking lunch for Scott Fitzgerald.'

DAY FIVE – Floating helplessly off the Azores.

DAY SIX – Floating helplessly off the Azores.

DAY SEVEN – Floating helplessly off the Azores.

FROM DAY SEVEN TO DAY TWENTY-THREE – Floating helplessly off the Azores.

DAY TWENTY-FOUR – Have decided to settle off the Azores.

DAY TWENTY-FIVE – Suddenly floating rapidly away from the Azores.

DAY TWENTY-SIX – Withdrawn application for permission to settle off the Azores.

DAY TWENTY-SEVEN – Captain acting strangely. 'This won't get us very far,' said McGonagall. 'What won't?'

said the Captain. 'This won't,' said McGonagall, holding up a piece of knotted string. 'Give me that,' said the Captain. 'I will not,' said William McGonagall.

DAY TWENTY-EIGHT – The Captain said 'Give me that string.'

DAY TWENTY-NINE – McGonagall said 'No.'

DAY THIRTY – Fighting broke out around the lifeboat between McGonagall and the Captain. 'This is mutiny,' they both shouted. 'One of us must be wrong,' said the Captain. 'Land ahoy,' shouted the lifeboat – and there, three inches away on a hot summers day, was the beach at Eastbourne, a pleasant resort, nestling on the South East coast, population 35,000 approx, and with the arrival of our heroes 35,000 plus two. There were regular trains to Victoria, and good connections by road to Brighton, Hailsham and Upper Dicker.

Good shopping Centre and a wide choice of hotels, The Excelsior being the widest, recommended by the AA (Alcoholics Anonymous).

As they landed McGonagall cried,

> Ooo Beautiful Town of Eastbourne
> A place where many people are born.
> Because it's a nice place to stay
> Not many people leave it to go away.
> And I and my Captain are grateful it is here,
> Because the moment we saw it we lost our fear,
> And there are trains every hour from the station.
> They go to Victoria and other parts of the nation.
> And soon we'll be travelling along the iron line,
> And I hope that during the journey I will feel
>   quite fine.

It was a new experience travelling in a dog crate in the guards van but the Captain seemed to know what he was doing. How he got into that crate of pigeons McGonagall would never know. But it was cheap and safe provided you could keep up the barking and cooing. 'I'm going to woof, miss all this, woof, when we get to London,' said McGonagall.

At Victoria station they broke open the pigeon crate and the Captain flew away, taking with him the vital insurance form for which McGonagall had suffered so much and now had nothing. 'Ah well, easy come, easy go,' he said. He threw himself under a train, and missed. It wasn't his lucky day.

'Do you do this often?,' said the wheel tapper. 'Not if you're successful,' said McGonagall, 'you should only need to do it once – does that answer your question?' and in one bound rejoined his wife and children in Edinburgh.

'Oh daddy's home, mummy,' said little Willie and little Sarah.

'Oh Willie dear you're back, your front, your legs and arms have all come home with you,' said Jeannie his wife.

'What's for dinner?,' he said.

'Breakfast,' said Jean. 'It's only six o'clock in the morning.'

'Ah, that's the sort of dinner I like,' he said throwing himself on the bed and missing it. 'Do you do this often?,' said the wheel tapper. 'I thought I'd answered your question,' said McGonagall.

'I'm sorry Willie, we sold the bed – Does that answer your question?' said Jean. 'Suddenly your £500 a week cheques were cut off.' 'But I never ever sent you any £500 a week cheques,' he said. 'I knew it was something like that,' she said. 'Does that answer your question?' he said. 'Willie, why are you in such a terrible ragged condition,' she said, 'with nae shoes and nae trews?' 'It's something to do with shortage of money. Does that answer your question?' he said. 'But dinnae worry, I'm going to start my career as an actor,' he said, 'first thing tomorrow morning

Ooh. lovely 6.24 train etc

On the Battlements of Kings Cross Station is the ghost of Hamlets Father

WHICH IS NOTHING TO DO WITH VICTORIA STATION AT ALL

as soon as I've had a good dinner.' 'That's no good to me,' said the wheel tapper. 'I'm to report to Wilton's Music Hall,' said McGonagall, 'the manager wishes to see me.' So a perfect evening came to a close in the McGonagall household. With a roaring candle in the grate McGonagall gathered his children and the wheel tapper around him and told them a traditional Scottish fairy story.

'Once upon a time there were three overdrafts . . .'

'I think I'll be off now,' said the wheel tapper. 'There's no work here.'

Extract from McGonagall's diary:

'Then next day Jeannie laundered my suit, boots, stick, hat and cape. As I sat naked by the fire I was concentrating deeply on my coming career, when suddenly everything went black and we didn't need to have the chimney swept for many a day.

It was a fearful task removing 8o lbs of soot from my body into a small hip bath, but once I'd got the hang of it it was quite enjoyable.

Starting with my feet I soon reached my neck when I beheld my black face suddenly in the mirror.

"Oh," I cried.

"Oh what?", said Jean.

"Othello," said I.

"Oh sod," said the wheel tapper, "there's no work here "Where's my penny Shakespeare Plays?" '

McGonagall composed a little tune called 'The Rattling Boy From Dublin Town' and played it to a musically crippled friend who could play the violin in the kneeling load position. He also occupied the chair of music at the University, which they had specially made to fit him.

'It's a nice tune' said the cripple.

'What do you think I should do with it?' said McGonagall.

'Take it to a garage,' said the cripple.

'Why?' said McGonagall.

'They'll drive it away for you,' said the cripple, 'and nobody need ever know.'

'But I don't want anyone else to drive it,' said McGonagall. 'It's only had one owner.'

'You mean it's still under guarantee?' said the surprised cripple.

'No it's under a tarpaulin in the garden.'

'What's it doing there?'

'It's waiting to be sung,' said McGonagall, then drawing on his last reserves of strength he said 'Goodbye, I must go.' One hour later he was on the stage at Wilton's Music Hall singing the theme song from Shakespeare's Macbeth. This had been a last minute change from his Othello act when a sudden squall had moved an entire week's soot from his face revealing an impostor.

'What are you going to do for us?' said the manager.

'Othello,' said McGonagall.

'But you're white,' said the manager.

'Can ye no turn the lights out?' said McGonagall.

The manager complied and McGonagall started his great act. From the crepuscular darkness came the sound 'Ooooooooo' followed by a pause, an agonized crash, and another 'Ooooooooooo.' He had fallen into the orchestra pit. 'Thank God, the concrete floor has broken my fall,' he said.

It had also broken his neck. But with one bound he was back on the stage and although in great pain he gave the following soliloquy. 'Ooooooh God, Aaaaaah Christ, the pain in ma' neek (trans. my neck). I cannae go to work like this.' So, for an hour screaming in agony, he stumbled round the darkened stage until a voice from

49

McGONAGALL AS JULIUS CAESAR

the gallery shouted 'What about Othello?' – 'Never mind about him,' said McGonagall. 'What about me?' and fell unconscious on the stage. As his body crashed to the floor he was given an ovation for the first time in his life. 'Encore,' they cried stamping their feet on the ground, but William McGonagall was resting. Unconscious, he was lifted to his feet by a kindly stage manager who hurled him back into the orchestra pit again. An enraged pianist hurled him back. An hour later the score was LOVE–40 in the manager's favour. McGonagall was only saved from another set by a Zeppelin raid on London during which he received a direct hit. It was a long time before McGonagall could play tennis again, but this did not stop his massive outpourings of poetry. Will anyone ever forget his immortal 'Ode to a Zeppelin raid over London'? – 'YES.'

'Just think Jeannie,' he said, 'the population of London is 8,000,000 and out of all of those, the Kaiser chose me. But on second thoughts,' he said 'it could have been ...' Here he stopped, a bus had run over him. He never composed in the middle of Regent Street again. Despite this surfeit of accidents to his person, which would have laid low lesser men, his fortitude and drive remained constant. For a year he never missed a day at the Finchley labour exchange where he recited his famous 'Poem of an Unemployed Genius in Finchley.'

> Oooooooohhh what a terrible thing is
>   Finchley unemployment,
> It stops lots of men's enjoyment,
> Standing in a queue day by day
> For one shilling and nine pence which is
>   the daily unemployment pay.
> But as the bus fare there is one and nine
> Things at the unemployment exchange are
>   not very fine.

> And it sends many a fine unemployed man
>> into a rage
> To have to go out to work to earn a decent
>> wage.

He said 'This is a fine poem, it could well be the corner-stone of the new working class socialist policies, I've a mind I'll tak it tae the Prime Minister of this fine island of ours.' He ran behind a 139 bus which took him to Downing Street. 'Evening all,' said a policeman, 'and just where are you a-going?'

'Tae see the Prime Minister,' said McGonagall.

'Have you made an appointment?' said the policeman.

'No, but I'm perfectly willing to,' said McGonagall.

'What is your business?'

'I have no business,' said McGonagall. 'I'm unemployed.'

'Why don't you get a job?' said the policeman.

'Oh no,' said McGonagall. 'I'll no take the easy way out.'

'Oh yes you will,' said the policeman and hurled him into the back of a police van, where he collided with a shadowy figure.

'I'm sorry, is that you dear?' said the figure.

'No dear,' said McGonagall, and added 'Who are you?'

'I'm the Prime Minister Mr Gladstone,' was the reply.

'Gladstone?' said McGonagall. 'Is that your bag on the seat?' 'No,' said Gladstone, 'It's Disraeli's. It's the money for the Suez Canal, he's buying it today and the bloke wants cash.'

Suddenly McGonagall stood up, banging his head on the roof.

> Ooooooooh Beautiful money for the Suez
>> Canal,
> For buying this for the British people
>> Disraeli has been a good pal.

Some people in their hearts, of interest shall
    not show a flicker,
But I tell you the wogs from India will get
    here much quicker.
They will benefit the economy of this land
By sweeping the gutters of Regent Street and
    the Strand.
In increasing numbers they'll come running
    to our shore,
And white noblemen like me won't have to
    work any more.
They'll drive every bus and tram and lorry,
And I for one will not be sorry.

'Who are you?' said Gladstone.

'A white nobleman,' said McGonagall, 'who won't have to work any more.'

'Is there anywhere we can drop you?' said Gladstone.

'Yes,' said McGonagall, 'anywhere.'

Gladstone dropped him over the side of Westminster Bridge.

'Oh dear,' said McGonagall as he plunged 120 ft towards the icy waters below. 80 ft further down it seemed that McGonagall was totally committed to entering the Thames. 'You'll be hearing from my solicitor in the morning,' he cried to Gladstone. 'It'll be better than listening to you,' shouted Gladstone. A little further down McGonagall met someone going the other way. 'You're breaking the law of gravity and you'll be arrested,' said McGonagall.

'No,' said the man, 'I'm not. I'm Adolf Saxe the Human Bullet and have but recently been fired from a cannon in Wapping.' 'Ah well you can always get another job,' said McGonagall. 'I was fired from Finchley Labour Exchange as unfit to be unemployed.' McGonagall braced himself for the icy shock of entering the water when SPLATT ... It was the friendly deck of a passing oil tanker. 'What's that mess of pottage doing on the poop-deck,' said the Captain. 'It's me,' said McGonagall. 'I bring you news from the Prime Minister. We've bought the Suez Canal, and this ship no longer has to go round the Cape.'

'I see,' said the Captain. 'I for one don't think it'll be a success.'

'Why not?' said McGonagall.

'We're going to Murmansk.'

'Well I'm not,' said McGonagall and got off.

'Man overboard,' shouted the Captain.

'So there is,' said the first mate carrying on with his dinner. McGonagall, using the powerful trudgeon stroke, made very little impression on the Thames. He did not realize this until a gentle voice from the shore shouted 'Welcome to France monsieur.' McGonagall quickly calculated that this marvellous stroke of fate had saved him

Train fare	£1	2. 11
Boat fare		18. 11
Pot of tea and biscuits in ships lounge		1. 9

His swim had therefore saved him a gross total of £2.3.7d. 'I'm rich,' he cried. 'I'll go first class to Paris.'

He walked the eighty miles in three days which was a first class effort.

CHAPTER V

'I think I'll sing a song in the Rue de la Paix,' he said. He did and felt much relieved. From then on for the next three weeks he lived in a hole in the ground on a vacant lot. Every morning he would get up and say 'Quelle bon jour?' which did him no good whatsoever, and it was suggested that he should move his residence. One winter's night as he lay wrapped in the Paris Soir, a gendarme approached him wearing Le Police Gazette and said, 'Bonjour – now move along or I will belt in zer nut.' 'But och aye Mr Gendarme the noo,' said McGonagall, ' 'tis Christmas the time of goodwill to all men.' 'Sacre bleu,' said the frog. 'Of course, a Merry Christmas to you mon ami, my friend, and your familie, may the goodness of the Christchild stay with you and your familie for evair, now move along before I belt in zer bloody nut.'

And strangely enough McGonagall moved on before zer nut was belted. McGonagall thought 'I must humour this man.' 'Oh mes cobblairs,' screamed the stricken gendarme as McGonagall's humorous boot went in. 'I like a man with a sense of humour,' said McGonagall, running away. 'So do I,' groaned the gendarme, 'where can we find one?' 'Leave it to me,' said McGonagall, 'I have a nose for these things.' 'I thought it was your boot,' said the gendarme. The bells of Notre Dame rang out. 'I'll get it,' said McGonagall, and he did, from Mlle Fifi La Jigajig who was well known for giving it.

He fell in love with her and she fell madly in love with his rent. He wrote these tender lines before he knew he had it:—

> Oooooh beautiful French Mademoiselle
> Who clutched me from the jaws of hell
> Away from the fiendish gendarme
> Who could have done me a great deal of harm.
> One blow from his truncheon so they say
> Could very easily put me away.
> While practising on the ground in case of that
>   dreadful blow
> Along came Mademoiselle Fifi and dragged me
>   from the snow.
> Since that day I've loved her with all my heart
> Which Albert Grollicks my butcher would say
>   was indeed the very best part
> It was being quoted at three francs per pound
>   on the open bourse
> And I'd like to point out that it wasn't *my* heart
>   of course.
> And every night now Fifi cooks me dinner
> But she's not giving me enough because
>   I keep getting thinner.

This poem of love and infatuation ended by McGonagall screaming from the waist downwards. The woman to whom he had devoted his life had been spicing his food with rat poison. Fortunately not being a rat he escaped with his life. But it had a worrying side effect — he started to die. In the Van Gogh Hospital for the Rat-Poisoned Poor, doctors worked on him day and night but he wouldn't part with a penny. Finally the doctors had a conference. 'It's no good,' said one, 'we shall have to cure him, and as quickly as possible, the banks close at four o'clock.'

Using a great heated copper enema they filled him with Fairy Liquid, Vim and Daz, Dettol, curried mangoes,

Bovril, Swoop, gum arabic, Brylcreem and Old Spice, increasing his value by 30 pounds and his body weight by 18 stone. They stood him on his feet, withdrew the enema and stood well back which apparently wasn't far enough. We will say no more of this matter owing to the large casualty list which included a two decker bus and a passing Bateau Mouche. At this stage the serious student will realize that McGonagall's life was running far from satisfactorily. In fact it had run so far from it that there he was without it, any questions? Let us examine his entire assets at this moment:

1 kilt (worn)	18s. od.
2 pairs underpants (very worn)	4s. 9d.
1 pair knitted tartan socks (odd)	2s. od.
3 vests (2 armless, 1 utterly harmless)	no quote available
1 Harris Tweed overcoat £3.12.0. o.n.o. also used as collateral on a house.	
1 Collateral on a house £3.12.0 also used as an overcoat.	
1 Dirk	£1.12.od. o.n.o.
1 Bogarde	open to offers
1 Meat Loaf Salad (only one owner)	9d.
1 Sporran (on loan)	£150
Insurance on family and house	1.0.od.
1 second-hand sword-dancers manual	1d. o.n.o.
1 100 ton rock belonging to his regiment, map reference African Ordnance Survey, long. 3428 lat. 6429, or c/o GPO Natal.	
1 Book of Scottish Reels	11d.
1 Reel of Scottish Books	11d.
60 Volumes of Pirbrook's Scottish Bagpipe Music	11d.
1 Truss inscribed from mother with love – sentimental value.	

Apart from the above he has part possession of a terraced house in MacGillikudy's Reeks, that part being three square feet under the sink, another three feet in the coal cellar, and the entire use of the rafters which he has let to his wife. As McGonagall said to her 'You never know,' and true to his word he never has.

He appeared for one night at the Moulin Rouge, deputizing for Le Petomain who was ill with stomach trouble. He managed one chorus of Annie Laurie and then had a trouser accident. 'The orchestra was too loud,' he cried as they slid him off the stage. 'I've not filled my contract,' raged McGonagall. 'That's the only thing you haven't filled,' said the manager and threw him out of the back door.

So ended the year for McGonagall on a sour note. As he packed his belongings in the dressing room, which he shared with Mr Spalls' bald performing pigeon he caught a glimpse of himself in the mirror, and there he was, aged fifty, with his bags packed, his kilt at a jaunty angle and a bald pigeon sitting on his head. 'You'll have tae find someone else's heed to sleep on tonicht lassie,' he said. It was just a microcosm of life. Carefully he took the cooing bird from his head and put it in the pressure cooker for dinner.

That night Mr Spalls went on the stage alone, and held up small empty perches and hoops, empty cages etc. crying 'Allez Oop'. He is now in a home for the insane at Aix en Provence, and McGonagall wasn't having it easy with Aix in the guts as the pigeon was tougher than he thought. What he hadn't realized was that the pigeon was really Mrs Spalls who was a master of disguise.

Here is an extract from a conversation between McGonagall and Mrs Spalls.

Mrs Spalls: 'What are you doing in my dressing room?'
McGonagall: 'Dressing room? What are you doing in my pressure cooker?'

McGONAGALL IN A DRAMATIC POSE
OF HIS OWN CHOOSING

Mrs S: 'I give up, what am I doing in your pressure cooker?'

McG: 'I think you ought to know you are doing an impression of pigeon pie.'

Mrs S: 'I think there must be some mistake.'

McG: 'Aye, and it would appear to be yours.'

Mrs S: 'What can I do to help?'

McG: 'Do an impression of an Irish Stew.'

Mrs S: 'How's this?'

Too late she realized the trap – McGonagall ate her. 'Delicious,' he said. 'I must write to your husband and congratulate him on your cooking.'

Straight away he wrote:

> Oooohhh beautiful woman who did an
>   impression of an Irish Stew,
> Who came along when I was feeling hungry
>   the noo.
> Let me assure you her brilliant impression was
>   nae in vain,
> But I had to eat her quickly before she could
>   change back again.
> She was the finest Irish Stew I have ever tasted,
> And it makes me sad to think of all those years
>   as a pigeon impressionist when she was wasted.
> Turning herself into a dinner was the finest
>   thing she has ever done,
> And apart from that for me it was lots of fun.
> There should be more women like her in the
>   Scottish nation,
> With people like her about there would be far
>   less starvation.
> And all thanks to her husband who really is a
>   brick,
> I am truly sorry that at this moment he is a silly
>   lunatic.
> I owe him an apology for eating his wife,

But even a lunatic must face up to the facts of
  life.
And one day when he's feeling better,
I'll send him a shilling postal order and a
  thank-you letter.

McGonagall, having lived life to the full decided to
go for the big-time, and as luck would have it the Gorilla
in the Paris Zoo died from Irish Stew poisoning, and
auditions were held the next morning. From all over
the world famous gorilla impersonators appeared, carrying their own skins. McGonagall watched, puzzled, as
gorillas leapt, swung, peeled bananas, bit keepers and
beat their chests, singing the while extracts from San-
ders of the River – unable to bear it any longer McGonagall shouted 'Stop the show. Those Gorillas are fakes –
Some of them are wearing shoes.' 'Of course,' said the
manager, 'wouldn't you if you'd had to walk here from
Africa?' McGonagall, 'Och no mon, if you'd wanted
Gorillas to come here from Africa, you could have got
real ones who could have swung all the way here without
touching the ground.'

'No, they cannot,' said the manager in French. 'The
trees stop at Gibraltar.'

'You are ze liar,' said McGonagall in Scottish.

'I'm no a liar,' said the manager in French. 'That's why
all those monkeys are stranded on the Rock the noo.'

'But they're not Gorillas,' said McGonagall.

'They were when they started,' said the manager.

'When I saw them they were only two foot tall,' said
McGonagall.

'That's because they weren't standing in trees,' said
the manager. 'It's the trees that give gorillas their extra
height.'

'In Africa you'll never see a self-respecting gorilla without a tree,' concluded the manager in an Irish accent to show that he was no fool himself.

'I notice you keep changing your accent,' said McGonagall.

'Jawohl,' said the manager, 'you see der police of five continents are after me.' 'What for?' said McGonagall. 'Because me poison honolable golilla with Ilish Stew in Palis Zoo,' said the manager in a Russian accent. 'Why are you blacking up?' said McGonagall. 'Cos Ah's on next Bwana,' and went straight into 'Massah's in the Cold Cold Ground.' 'My God, so he killed him as well' thought McGonagall. 'He'll no get me into his deadly clutches.'

The next day the big attraction at the Paris Zoo was a gorilla wearing a kilt and shoes shouting 'Help, help, I am a prisoner in a gorilla skin.' Whereupon he leapt on to a log and declaimed to the world,

> Oooooohhh Twas on the third of June in
>   the Year 1882
> A terrible French confidence trick was
>   played on William McGonagall the noo.
> He was incarcerated in a gorilla skin and
>   chained up a tree
> And the reason for this as far as he's concerned
>   is very hard to see.
> He wrote to the British Ambassador and told
>   him of this crime,
> He wrote 'I'd love to come and help you but
>   I don't have the time.'
> Meanwhile a captive gorilla arrived at the
>   zoo in a terrible rage,
> And in order to keep him happy they put
>   him in McGonagall's cage.
> When he caught sight of McGonagall he
>   seemed to go out of his mind,

> He didn't seem to think of him as one of his
>   own kind.
> He grabbed him by the ankle and smashed
>   him to the ground
> Which made all the people laugh for many
>   miles around.

At a local Gorilla Hospital a surgeon asked, 'How long have you been playing zis silly game?' as he removed McGonagall from the gorilla skin. 'I would say it was approximately days three, but to me it felt like years nine, I did ask the British Ambassador but he replied, "I don't have the time".' 'There, there' said the great French Gorilla surgeon as he removed the last bits of McGonagall from the skin. 'What's that heap of stuff on the flae*?' asked McGonagall 'That's you!' said the surgeon. 'From now on you must take things quietly.' So he did. He became a pickpocket.

One simple question from a gendarme finished his career.

'Wot are you doink wiz ze French Crown Jewels in zat sack marked "Swag"?' 'I need notice of that question' said McGonagall and took one step backwards and fell in the Seine. 'Quelle bonne chance' said the gendarme, putting on a red comic nose, 'I have waited twenty years to make zis joke' and shouted at the disappearing McGonagall 'You are in-Seine'.

* floor

McGONAGALL FLOATING DOWN THE SEIN

CHAPTER VI

Dear reader, we have so far covered McGonagall's life from his birth until the moment when he was pronounced insane by a gendarme wearing a false red nose. It was the gendarme who looked more suspiciously insane. Picture the scene – A mature Scottish poet floating downstream clutching a sack of Imperial Jewels in no way suggests insanity, whereas a French gendarme in his prime wearing a false red nose suggests a fair degree of mental instability, but we leave it to the reader to make the choice. One bystander was heard to remark, 'Look – there is the Scottish branch of the Bonaparte Dynasty enjoying the waters of the city and carrying the Crown Jewels in the event of a sudden restoration of the Monarchy.' But the strange thing is that self-same spectator was heard to make exactly the same statement about the red-nosed gendarme, thus giving the reader the choice of a third lunatic.

Our own personal choice is Mrs Ada Scrackle, The Millstone, Piles Road, Crappington, Berks. Her speciality was sleeping nude inside a grand piano while her husband played the Marseillaise on the spoons. Alas for some inexplicable reason while he was at work, she exploded leaving a great gap in his life and in the kitchen ceiling. He took the bits round to a friend of his who was very clever with his hands (about which time McGonagall was about a mile off Deauville).

The friend said 'I'm sorry, I'm no longer very clever with my hands but watch this.' He took off his boots and on the remains of Mrs Scrackle he played the 'Eroica' Symphony with his feet. The husband realized that all these years he had been married to Ludwig van Beethoven and had been living a lie.

AS NAPOLEON

Now read on:

Those of you, on a very foggy morning in 1900, standing on the Deauville sands, would have heard the following coming from out of the sea mist:

> Ooooooooooohhhhh . . . What a terrible thing
> is the English Channel Sea.
> If I stay in it much longer it will be the death of
> me
> Oooh for one sip of a glass of hot toddy.
> Which would warm my hands, feet and legs and
> other parts of my body.
> But it's no guid thinking of fancy things like that
> I'm glad I came out in my overcoat and a hat.
> But hark, what is this sound I hear approaching
> me
> CRUNCH, THUD and CHRIST – I've been
> hit by a ship from the Queen's Navee.
> After this mighty 30,000 ton leviathan had stove
> in my chest,
> They pulled me aboard and the Captain said,
> 'I'll do the rest'.
> 'No,' I said 'not while I'm feeling so tired,
> 'This isn't the job for which I was hired.'
> The bosun said 'Give us lads a show on the after
> deck,
> 'They won't mind even though you look such a
> wreck'.

That night McGonagall triumphed as he blacked up with hot tar to do Othello, and the men said they'd never seen anything like it before. The cook summed it up best by saying, 'There's no bluidy food for that idiot'. As a reward the captain gave him the freedom of the scuppers where he slept every night. The captain broke out the plague flag. McGonagall was guilt-stricken and wrote,

Dear Monsieur the President in Paris,

By now you will have read in the paper that the French Crown Jewels have been stolen. I stole them and now wish to return them. You will find them at map reference Longitude 360, Latitude 423, at a depth of 160 fathoms.
(and so saying he threw the jewels over the side)
He finished the letter:

Your chum
Willie
Poet & Jewel Thief

Currently appearing this week After Deck HMS *Dreadnought* – Next week The Ada Scrackle Memorial Theatre, Piles Road.

As the giant battleship sailed under the giant structure McGonagall asked the captain, 'What's that?' 'The Forth Bridge' he replied. 'Why do they call it the Forth Bridge?' asked McGonagall. 'Because the other three fell down,' said the Captain and went on, 'I waited twenty years to tell that joke – help me off with this red nose.'

Great cheering crowds lined the dockside. 'I thought I told you to keep my presence secret' said McGonagall to the Captain. The crowds were in fact starving porters, unemployed these hundred years since the last passenger ship had docked there. Every day, seven days a week they had waited there with the trolleys, and to fill in time they wheeled each other about. Now, although weakened by a hundred years unemployment, they rallied at the sight of the great ship.

'Luggage, Luggage' they screamed as they poured up the gang plank, over the gunwhales and down into the bowels of the ship. In half an hour the ship was stripped of everything, loaded onto a train and driven off at a high speed to the Midlands where an amazed station master was told, 'There's a battleship just pulling into platform nine' – 'It's all this rain we've been getting' he said.

McGonagall did well on the deal. He and the Captain

sold the skeleton of the battleship to the Natural History Museum, who in turn sold it to the Navy as a battleship.

With the proceeds of the sale McGonagall returned home to his wife. He threw three pounds on the table and said, 'There dear, I told you I'd make my fortune.'

The happy couple spent the rest of the day counting and recounting the three pounds but alas it never came to any more. 'We'll have to settle for three pounds' said McGonagall. 'I'll settle for three pounds' said Jean, 'You go and find something to settle for yourself.'

'Och, a mon has tae du what a mon hast tae du' said McGonagall and went and did it in the garden.

'God knows where he does it' said Jean, 'for we havenae got a garden.'

McGonagall spent the next week doing odd jobs around the house, which Jean was forced to clean up.

'How are the children?' said McGonagall. 'I'm glad you've noticed they're not here' said Jean. 'Yes I'm rather glad I've noticed that too' said McGonagall, pocketing the three pounds that Jean had left carelessly on the table. 'Yes' said Jean, 'Willie is in the Irish Guards.' 'But he's only four' said McGonagal. 'D'you think it was easy?' said Jean, 'night after night teaching him to walk on stilts.' 'What about wee Annie?' said McGonagall. 'She's in the Irish Guards too' said Jeannie. 'But she's a girl, what's she doing?' said McGonagall. 'Willie's standing on her shoulders' said Jeannie. 'Their money comes in handy' she said. 'Mine comes in envelopes' said McGonagall. At that moment – there was a ragged knock at the door. 'I'll get it' said Jean. 'No I'll get it' said McGonagall, 'you've already had it.'

He opened the door – framed there was a living skeleton, bald, toothless and clad in the remains of something, but otherwise had everything going for him, including the dog. 'Don't laugh' said the spectre. 'Who are you?' said

McGonagall. 'I'm your landlord' it replied, 'and it should be pretty obvious to you that we are going to have to put your rent up.' 'Up where?' said the innocent McGonagall. 'Don't sod about' said the spectre, 'I'm starving.' 'I understand' said McGonagall, 'how much?' 'Would you believe three pounds?' it said. 'Three pounds? That's my entire fortune' said McGonagall. 'Well it's now your misfortune' said the spectre, holding out a begging bowl marked TORY CENTRAL OFFICE COLLECTOR NO. 64. 'Your move.'

'Right' said McGonagall, stepping backwards and slamming the door.

'Your move now' shouted McGonagall.

'I've moved' said a voice behind him. He turned – it was the spectre.

'How do you do that?' said McGonagall.

'If I knew do you think I'd be a starving landlord?' said the spectre.

The door opened and there stood an Irish Guardsman. 'The kids are home, Jean' said McGonagall. 'Daddy' said Willie, dismounting from his sister's shoulders. The phantom watched horrified as the jacket leapt off the trousers. 'My God' said the landlord. 'No it's not, it's my two children' said McGonagall. 'If they're in the Irish Guards what are they doing here?' said the spectre.

'They're deserting' said McGonagall. 'So am I' said the spectre, 'I've had enough.'

'Had enough what?' said McGonagall, 'you haven't eaten a thing. I should know I've been watching you.'

'All right then I'm going to demand my just dues' said the Landlord.

'Some of my best friends are just Jews' said McGonagall.

At that moment the skies were split asunder by thunder and forked lightning came through the cardboard roof of the house to strike the phantom landlord dead. 'Just my bloody luck' he said and expired, leaving McGonagall with a funeral bill of three pounds. 'God works in mysterious ways' said McGonagall. 'I wish he'd work our way' said Jean, boiling two pieces of lino for the children's tea. 'Oh yum yum, lino for tea' said McGonagall who didn't know any better.

> Oooooooohhhh beautiful piece of lino being
> braised for my tea,
> The very thought of it sends the gastric juices
> running round me.
> My boots have often walked across you on the
> floor
> And I know when I've had some, I will want
> some more.
> And now the lino has almost gone you see
> So it'll be curtains for breakfast, and curtains
> for me.

'Willie' said Jean, 'your poetry has improved beyond all recognition.'

'So that's why nobody recognizes it' said McGonagall. 'What I need Jean' he said 'is Royal patronage, you can't get anywhere without it.'

'I just went upstairs without it' said Jean coming down again.

'If I could only get into Her Majesty's proximity, I could sway her with the power of my verse' said McGonagall. 'I could be her Svengali, and she could be my Trilby, or preferably my Glengarry.'

CHAPTER VII

Next day at the Dundee Labour Exchange, which he was attending to receive his twentieth anniversary unemployment award, he was approached by a dignified man wearing a Windsor Tartan and a Trilby. It was Mr Svengali, (a well-known practical joker and amateur greengrocer). He was clutching a five string banjo. 'I could not but hear you bemoaning your fate' he said, 'but I happen to have Royal contacts.' 'I didn't know she wore them' said McGonagall who had waited twenty years to tell the joke.

'Let me take that red nose from your face and we'll talk business' said Svengali. 'If you wish to read poetry to Her Majesty Queen Victoria while she is on the throne I have here a letter of introduction.'

Armed with this letter McGonagall prepared for his great march to Balmoral. He packed Two Crommocks, a Crinkie, a Crillick and a MacGrackie, several gwirndles, a Toley, a small sack of Killiekrankie, $\frac{1}{2}$ pint of milk and a packet of Stork margarine because he couldn't tell the difference. To keep out the bitter cold of the hielands he lagged his legs. He put on eight sweaters, four pairs of woollen under pants, gloves, a highland raglan coat, and shetland earplugs. Puzzled wayfarers watched as this heavily clad figure, pouring with sweat, struggled down the road on this boiling hot summer's day, gasping 'Water, water'.

·'I think he's trainin' for his death' said an elderly sage.

'Aye and I think he's nearly there' said another.

Up the side of Ben Nevis he went o'er the MacReekie plateau, round the Laing Dangle, and through Mrs Agnes McWhirtle's front room, straight into the gloaming. 'We've seen the last of him' said Mrs Agnes McWhirtle. She was quite wrong because at that moment he came back in through the side door. 'It's a mite cold oot there' he said. 'Could I have a bed and board for the nicht?' 'No' she said, 'but I could let you have a board for a bed.' 'How much will that be?' said McGonagall. 'Would you believe three pounds?' said a spectre stepping from a dark doorway. 'It's the phantom landlord' gasped McGonagall. 'Can I give you a pound on account?' 'On account of what?' 'On account of I haven't got any more' said McGonagall.

'I'm off' said the wheel tapper, 'there's no work here.'

'Where are you going?' said McGonagall.

'Balmoral.'

'Can you gie us a lift?'

'A lift won't get you to Balmoral – that only goes up and down, what you need is a form of conveyance that goes forwards or backwards, preferably the latter' said the wheel tapper.

'What do you mean?' said McGonagall.

'I don't know, I'm only a wheel tapper.'

'Let *me* help you on your way' said the spectre, and, slipping a noose over McGonagall's head, pulled his feet clear of the floor.

'This is not the way to Balmoral' said McGonagall.

'You're too clever for me' said the spectre lowering him to the ground.

'We'll put him up for the night' said Mrs McWhirtle, 'I'll show ye to your chamber.' And so she did. There it was under the bed. With a candle roaring in the fireplace McGonagall settled down for a comfortable night. He thought of Jean and the children. Then he thought of the children without Jean. He then thought of himself, Jean and the children. He then thought of Jean and himself, without the children. He then thought of Jean with one child, but without him and the other. He thought of the other child alone with Jean, him, and the first child. He then thought of the first child and himself without Jean, with the other child not there. He then thought of nothing at all with an uncle in the background. He brought the uncle forward with Jean and the two children. He thought of the wheel tapper who said, 'I'm off there's no work here.'

Mrs McWhirtle opened the door and said 'You're going to be cold in the night.' 'What makes you think that?' said McGonagall. 'We're putting you in the garden, we need the room' she said. 'What for?' said McGonagall. 'Airing' she said, 'the neighbours are complaining about the smell.' 'I don't have to take this from you' said McGonagall. 'Oh yes you do' said Mrs McWhirtle, and Kung

ON HIS WAY TO
BALMORAL

Fu'd him through the window. He spent a restless night in a tree. At dawn he set off for Balmoral and the milestone said '130 miles to Balmoral'. 'Why don't you shut up' said McGonagall.

No words could describe the agonizing journey to Balmoral as taken by McGonagall. It took two long years; you see for the first year and a half he was going the wrong way. One can imagine McGonagall's agony when he finally reached the walls of the great castle and cried, 'Beloved Queen, are you in?' 'No, but I am' said a dark-skinned gentleman named Mr Singis Thing. 'I've got the place on a long lease. Things haven't been going too well with H.M., there's a rumour that Philip and Her are opening an agency called Rent-a-Prince, meantime I'm keeping the castle going on curry. At this very moment She and Philip and Ann are having a Chicken Binda-loo and if you open the door you can hear the screams. Mark's been in the karzi for half-an-hour, but still as I said to the Prime Minister, "How are things?" and he replied "Things are picking up", and goodness gracious next time I saw him there he was in the street picking up

(past chis)

Mac O O O O O O ᴏ ᴏ ᴖ

McGONAGALL GOING THROUGH
LEWISHAM

things. Come back to No. 10 I've got a room full of it.'
'Nae' said McGonagall, drawing his kilt around him revealing just the tip, 'if the auld country is in trouble I must
take my part to help restore her to her former greatness.'
He struck a dramatic poetic prose and commenced

> 'Oooooooooooohhhh', (which cleared the street
>   in three seconds flat).
> 'Twas in the year of January in the month of
>   1883,
> That the beautiful country of England was
>   having a hard time ye see.
> Because the Prime Minister Mr Gladstone
>   was picking up things in the streets,
> And taking them home to the children and
>   passing them off as sweets;
> And poor old Queen Victoria had let her house
>   to the wogs
> Who had started a pet food factory, using
>   chopped up royal cats and dogs.
> That's why all over the country the flags are
>   flying at half mast
> For all those doggies and pussy cats who will
>   shortly be breathing their last.
> But do not worry dear reader for the truth is
>   clear and plain
> And soon the green lanes of England will be
>   covered in dogshit again.'

Hardly had this poem fallen from his lips than the
Stock Exchange Index soared as never before. Deep
Frozen Pussy Cats Ltd. increased by 90 shillings a share.
International Mongrel Trappers went up £2. Imported
Disguised Wog Cooks Inc. reached an all time high, and
Royal Balmoral Curries went ahead. So did McGonagall,
he had little alternative, with a howling mob behind
him, throwing rocks, he was seen safely to the city gates,
which were locked.

'What now?' you may cry, as did McGonagall, only louder. Suddenly a great idea occurred to him – 'HELP' he shouted. A rock bounced off his skull, it wasn't such a good idea after all. When he came to he was lying on a pussy cat conveyor belt in a Curried Pet Food Factory, minus his kilt. 'Bad luck' said a gentle voice above him, 'he's come to.' McGonagall looked up in time to see a man put down a meat cleaver. 'Where's ma kilt?' said McGonagall. 'I'll have it for you in a moment' said the Kosher butcher opening a can of tinned kilt for the American Export market. 'Thanks laddie' said McGonagall strapping it round his waist, 'and under the circumstances I think you must agree that sounds pretty generous – and noo ma legs.'

It was a tired McGonagall who crawled into a telephone box to phone in his mighty ode to Queen Victoria.

QUEEN VICTORIA: Hello? – Queen Victoria speaking and I'm very big in England.

MCGONAGALL: Good morning Quin, you dinae ken me but I'm a great fan of yours and my daughter would like your autograph, and I'm very big in Scotland. I've just got off the twenty-five to eleven train at Liverpool Street.

QUEEN: Good.

MCGONAGALL: Why?

QUEEN: I'm still on it.

MCGONAGALL: Ah well Quin we've all got to be on something even if it's only a train.

QUEEN: It may be only a train to you but to me it's Balmoral Castle.

STATION MASTER: The train now arriving at Platform 2 is Balmoral Castle.

QUEEN: You're on a crossed line.

STATION MASTER: I know which line I'm on, I pulled the points.

78

It was a puzzled crowd which watched a red telephone box leave from Platform 1 and proceed along the line to Balmoral. From inside it came the following poem:

> Oooooooooooh beautiful red telephone box
>   travelling down the silvery railway line,
> If it keeps it up by tonight I will be in Newcastle
>   on Tyne
> And to me that will be a terrible blow
> Because that is not the destination to which
>   I wish to go.
> At which time I flashed past a man looking very
>   neat and dapper,
> He was shouting, 'I'm off there's no work here',
>   it was my old friend the wheel tapper
> He was also shouting, 'you're lucky to be alive'.
> I was about to say 'Why?' when I was struck
>   head-on by the ten forty five.

The scene is the wrecked 2.30 telephone box beside the line in a coal siding in Dumfries. 'Oooooooooh' groaned McGonagall, at which moment the phone rang. The shattered wreck called McGonagall raised the phone to his ear, 'Hello Liverpool Street Exchange?' said McGonagall. 'I've got to say something' he thought. 'It's for you' he said, passing it to the wheel tapper. 'And this' said the wheel tapper bringing his hammer down on McGonagall's teeth 'is for you, I'm off' he said, 'there's no work here.'

A pyjama clad dentist forced a pair of dog's false teeth into the mouth of a late customer. 'How's that?' he said. 'Woof, woof' said McGonagall. 'That'll be five guineas' said the dentist. 'Woof, woof' stalled McGonagall and ran down the stairs barking. 'I'm nae giving in to that kind of price,' he thought, 'and where can a puir wee dog find 5 guineas at this time of night?' 'There's work here' shouted McGonagall. With one bound the wheel tapper was be-

side him. 'Where?' he said. 'It's these teeth' said McGonagall, 'can you take two inches off the top set so that people
can see in, and I can see out?' 'No I can't' said the wheel
tapper, 'I got on at Colchester cos there's no work there.'

CHAPTER VIII

THE SCENE: The Gabes Oasis in Tunisia.

CHAPTER IX

'Where have you been?' said McGonagall. 'Now you won't believe this' said the wheel tapper, 'but I've just been to the Gabes Oasis and there's no work there either. Do you think I'm in the wrong job?' 'Why, what are you?' said McGonagall. 'I'm really a dental mechanic' said the wheel tapper 'and I can fix you up with a new set of teeth.' And he did. McGonagall was well pleased, and bit him. 'They're working real well' he said. 'Will you be needing these old dog's false teeth?' said the wheel tapper. 'Nae' said McGonagall. 'I'm giving them up for Lent.' 'Do you mean I can keep them?' said the wheel tapper. 'I see no reason why not' said McGonagall. 'Very well' said the wheel tapper, 'in that case I will take it from what you have said that the teeth have irrevocably transferred into my possession, and in no way can you make any legal claim even should your present teeth be considered persona non grata – whereas subject to strikes, lockouts, floods, acts of God, typhus, volcanic upheavals, piles and other diseases of the gums, they are insured as an inheritance to be bequeathed in the event of my death to my wife, ex-Tsarina of Russia decd., now living under the assumed name of Fred Mogglers, c/o The Refined Wrestlers Luncheon Counter, Potters Bar. Of course there will be moments during an equinox of the moon when these teeth could be made available to needy dogs, but then only until sunset, after which the dogs could be

**McGONAGALL WORKING WITH DOG'S
FALSE TEETH**

liable to be arrested, shot, hung and deported for wrongful possession of teeth. Would you just sign here, here, here, here and here' said the wheel tapper, flicking the pages of a cheque book.

'This is a cheque for a million pounds' said McGonagall. 'Yes' said the wheel tapper. 'It's better than a cheque for £4.10. – sign here' he said, pointing towards a labour exchange. Carefully McGonagall wrote across the bottom 'Lord Niffington Clunt or Something'.

The next morning from a debtors prison Lord Niffington Clunt or Something was trying to explain to his bank manager, who was in the next cell, why his account had fallen by a million pounds overnight. 'How would I know?' said the bank manager, 'I've been in here fourteen years.'

'What are you in for?' asked Clunt. 'Well' said the bank manager (who was roasting a prison rat over a match), 'I went into the police station to report the loss of my pussy cat and one of the older sergeants recognized me.' 'That smells lovely' said Lord Clunt as the flavour of the roasting rat wafted through the bars of his cage. 'Yes it is, and that's all you're bloody well getting' said the bank manager.

So ended another pleasant day in Newgate prison. No it didn't, suddenly a bundle of rags was hurled into Lord Clunt's cage. 'Is that lunch?' said Lord Clunt. 'No' said the warden, 'it's William McGonagall.' 'Don't eat me all at once' said McGonagall, 'I've got a wife and four kids, save some from them.' 'I wouldn't harm a hair of your head' said Clunt taking a bite out of his foot. 'Stand well back' said McGonagall. 'There's some mistake.' 'You're right' said Clunt, 'it's underdone. Warden I want to make a complaint.' The warden opened the cell door and in one bound McGonagall was free. 'I must get ma poems up tae ma Queen before they drop in value and while the fire of

P. Sethos

THE STAG AT BAY

youth is still in ma kilt.' With a merry whistle and a wee flick of the sporran he swung into a fine Hie'land March, April, May and June. He returned home to his wife and children and demanded a roast rat sandwich – a trick he had learnt in Newgate Prison.

While he waited he read the tablecloth.

The Times Court Circular (what a funny shape he thought). *Situations Vacant*. He felt the fear of wages come over him. Since a child he had tried to avoid the dreaded 'working-for-a-living' but *there* was the tantalizing call of the big time. He took a pull from his hip flask, one from his knee flask, two from his elbow flask, and finally one from his ankle flask. He noticed on the way down that he was inside leg 43, whereas formally he was inside leg 32 – it had been a long hard pull. 'I didn't recognize the old place' he said as he passed it on the way up. He ran his fingers down the list of Sits. Vac.

WANTED: Admiral of the Fleet (Nae he hadn't enough water for that).

WANTED: Temporary Window Box Superintendent (Nae he didn't have enough water for that either – but it reminded him of the day he tried to sell some of his own land. The potential purchaser – a certain Mr Harry H had arrived. 'I saw your advert in the Jewish Chronicle' he said, 'for the sale of a piece of land overlooking the highlands.' McGonagall took him through his house which was all in the same room and pointed to a window box. 'A £1,000' he said. Harry H reeled backwards. 'It's too small' he said. 'Too small?' said McGonagall, 'it used to have a herd of spotted deer on it'.

'What happened?'

'They fell off'.

'Where are they now?'

'I do not nae, they haven't been spotted since – they

are now the only herd of unspotted deer in Turkey.' 'I
thought you said they were in Scotland.'
'They were but they fell off –'
H thought, 'This man is an idiot.' At exactly the same
moment McGonagall was thinking the same thing. 'I
can get this plot of land for a song' thought H and
burst into 'My Yiddisha Momma.' 'That's nae gude –
it's the wrong song' said McGonagall, 'I'll only settle
for Beethoven's Fifth Symphony.' 'Right, boys' shouted
H, 'bring in the piano' and immediately went in to
the first stirring notes, 'Dum Dum Dum Dum.' 'Any
advance on "Dum Dum Dum Dum"' shouted McGonagall from his auctioneer's rostrum. 'Titty titty tum titty
tum' said a filthy one-legged creature strapped to the
back of a yak. 'Any advance on "Titty titty tum titty
tum?"' shouted McGonagall from the stage of Covent
Garden. 'What are you doing here?' asked a puzzled
lead tenor. 'I thought you were going to make a bid'
said McGonagall. 'So I am' said the tenor and burst into
'Largo factotum un bella citta largo.'
'Sold to Largo Factotum for a tenner' said McGonagall.
Whereupon the tenor gave him a score – Arsenal 3-
West Indies – all out for 2. 'I must go now' said Mc-
Gonagall 'as I am running my fingers down the sits.
vac. column of the Court Circular.'

WANTED: Chambermaid.

WANTED: Part time Lord Chancellor (own money essential).

WANTED: Keeper of the Royal Karzi (own bucket
essential).

WANTED: Combined Jester and Court Cripple (own
hump) – 'Nae, I haven't enough water for that' thought
McGonagall.

WANTED: One Royal Camel (no hump) on loan to Royal

Cripple. Then came the entry which made his heart tremble.

WANTED: A stand off John Brown, the current John Brown being laid low with a stroke. 'That must be a stroke of luck, especially for me' said McGonagall.

THE BALL OF KERRIEMUIR
(where you cannot see the carpet)

CHAPTER X

The sun was pouring with rain that morning as McGonagall pushed his tricycle towards Balmoral Castle. 'I have
a mind to save fuel' he puffed. He knocked at the main
gate. 'No hawkers, no circulars' cried a voice from within.
'I have no hawks and I am not circular' said McGonagall,
'does that answer your question?' The door swung open
outwards hurling him into the moat. 'He's gone' said
the voice of the combined sergeant namely a girl standing on a little boy's shoulders, both being one and a half
lance-corporals each. It was the McGonagall children
back on duty. 'Father?' cried the combined sergeant. 'I
cannae gae any farther' cried McGonagall, 'I'm right at
the bottom.' 'It suits you,' said the combined sergeant. 'Is
the Quinn in?' said McGonagall. 'The Queen is in unless
she's staying there' said the combined sergeant. 'I dinnae
ken' said McGonagall.

'There is no dinner Ken' said the combined sergeant
who had mistaken him for 'Dinner' Ken MacGregor the
Moat Pervert. 'Get the hoses on him' said the Prince
Consort. 'Are you the Prince Consort?' said McGonagall.

'Jawohl!'

'I didn't think you had enough water for that.'

'Ja would you like to come up unt see it?'

'Aye' said McGonagall, 'it's a fine collection of water
you have here. Why do ye keep it up here on the fourth
floor?'

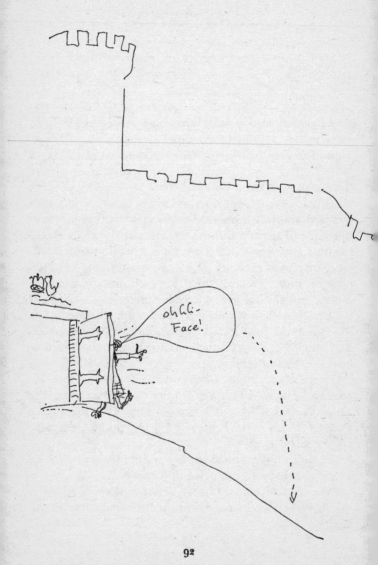

'It is for mein deer in zer vindow boxess.'

A woman came in wearing a white handkerchief held under the chin with an elastic band, and topped with a silver pepper pot.

'Who am I' she said.

'Unless I'm very much mistaken' said the Prince Consort, 'you are Her Imperial Majesty Victoria. Dei. Gra. Britt. Regina. Fid. Def. Ind. Imp.'

'You heard that Your Majesty?' said McGonagall, 'you are a Deaf Imp from India and you should be glad that we have given you asylum.'

'Oh yes' said a white coated figure stepping out of a bowl of fruit, 'this castle is one of the finest asylums in the world, ask any of the deaf imps from India staying here.'

'Pardon?' said McGonagall, cupping his ear.

'It must be contagious,' said the white coated man cupping *His* ear.

'Vat are you both sayink?' said Albert cupping both ears.

'My God, it's getting worse' said the white coated man, cupping both ears, his nose and his teeth.

'Now' said the Queen, mounting the throne and galloping round the room and over McGonagall, trampling him into the carpet, 'What did you come about?'

'I came about half-past one your Majesty, but I was held up by the moat, it was an hour late leaving. I should like to apply for the vacant John Brown position.'

'That's the one you're in now' said the Queen, galloping over him again.

'You mean I've got the job?'

'Arise Vacant John Brown. Welcome to Balmoral.'

'You're welcome to it too' he said.

Suddenly a great flash of lightning lit the sky and a torrential storm broke out.

'Quick, a drink, Albert' said the terrified Queen.

'Here drink this' he said forcing a bottle of port down her throat.

'It tastes terrible' said Def. Imp.

'I should have opened the bottle.'

'Och weel, any old port in a storm' said McGonagall making a joke. He observed the Prince Consort, cupped his ear, filled it with wine and drank it.

'You'll like it here' said the man in the white jacket.

'Who are you?' said McGonagall.

'I was hoping you might be able to tell me that' said the man.

'I think you are an unemployed wheel tapper hiding inside a lunatic asylum attendant.'

'Curses' said the wheel tapper, 'and I thought my disguise was perfect.'

'Get out' said the white coated attendant, 'I want to go to lunch and I can't afford two dinners.'

'Blimey, I'm off' said the wheel tapper, 'there's no lunch here.'

McGonagall struck a poetic pose, 'Ooooooooooooooooo'

'Quick, everybody out' said Albert, 'he's going to poem any moment.'

'Oooooooooooooooooooooooooh . . .'

'Not on my carpet' said the Queen, 'it's an expensive Afghanistan with 16,000 silk threads per square inch, loomed by hand by 24 generations of Royal Carpet Weavers whose new single comes out this week.'

'We must be standing on the B side' said McGonagall.

'And I'm off to the C side' said the wheel tapper rolling up his trousers and knotting a white handkerchief round his head.

'Ooooooooooooohhhooooooo' continued McGonagall

> Beautiful Afghanistan Carpet belonging to
>   the Quinn
> Is one of the finest things on which I've
>   ever been

> Chorus
> Whack fal de da, fal de darelido
> Whack fal de da, fal de darelay
> Whack fal de da, fal de darelido
> Whack fal de da, fal de darelay

> Ooooooooooooooooooohhh
> Beautiful Afghanistan Carpet which still
>   belongs to the Quinn
> It's still one of the finest things on which

95

I've ever been [singing]
>Whack fal de da, etc. (as above)

Ooooooooooooooooohhh
Beautiful Afghanistan Carpet on which
>three times I've been
I'm not standing on it any more as they've
>sent it for a dry clean.

[singing]
>Whack fal de da, etc. (as above)

'Put the hoses on him' said the Prince Consort. This is not one of McGonagall's best poems although on reflection it was; and on further reflection it was the worst bloody thing he had ever written.

That night in honour of McGonagall the Queen threw a magnificent dinner which hit him full in the face,

'OOOOoooooooooohhh
Magnificent dinner thrown by Queen Victoria,
You caught me full in the face before I even
>saw yer.

Although it is a great honour to be hit by
  Imperial Food,
If it had been thrown by an ordinary person I
  would have said 'That's rude'.
But this haddock and prunes clinging to my
  chest,
Because it's from the Royal kitchen it is only
  of the best.
Gratefully I ate fish and prunes in pounds
  cwts and tons
And the next day I had fish poisoning
  accompanied by the runs.

Following this McGonagall had an attack of depression. He visited Sir Ralph Fees the famous Harley Street Depression who on seeing McGonagall immediately attacked him, saying – 'This is an attack of depression, 5 guineas please. Will you please pay the nurse on your way out.' 'I demand a second opinion' said McGonagall. 'Right, I'll give it you, you're suffering from an attack of depression' said Sir Ralph. 'What does that mean?' said McGonagall. 'That means another 5 guineas' said Sir Ralph. 'Take your clothes off and lay on the couch' he said.

Seeing the pale wraith-like, waxen figure with tufts of red hair, hither, thither, everywhere, the great Sir Ralph Fees could not believe his eyes, he also could not believe his ears, nose and throat, such was the terrible condition of McGonagall. He quickly ran his stethoscope over McGonagall's wallet. 'My God' he said, 'I must get you to a bank as soon as possible.'

'You'll need this' he said putting a loaded pistol into McGonagall's hand. 'I want you to point it at the bank teller and read from this card.'

Half-an-hour later McGonagall was standing in the bank pointing a pistol at Mr Anthony Smithbrownjonesrobinsonwhiteblackgreenultramarinechurchillmacdonaldbaldwinlloydgeorgewilsonheathfumanchunisonbismarkarchipelagoorangessixpenceapound – Smith by which time the police had arrived and he was arrested.

'Have you got a licence for that gun?' said a peeler.

With great presence of mind McGonagall answered, 'No'. Then added, 'I am a poet.'

'Can I see your poetic licence then?' said the peeler.

Again, with great presence of mind, McGonagall said, 'Pardon?'

'You'll pay for this' said the peeler.

'Nonsense' said McGonagall, 'that was a free pardon' and so saying walked out a free man.

FULL FRONTAL McGONAGALL

'Just a minute' said the peeler, 'I've seen through your ruse, and I believe you to be a bankrobber which entitles you to wear these for the next six months.'

So saying he clamped a pair of handcuffs on McGonagall, but his wrists were so thin that the handcuffs fell off.

'Quick' shouted the peeler leaping onto McGonagall's head, 'he's trying to escape.'

'Come down' said McGonagall to the peeler on his head 'and let me explain.'

'What a view from up here' said the peeler, 'do you know I can see the Hog's Back? I can also see the Cat's Legs and the Dog's Belly.'

'You can't fool me' said McGonagall, 'you are using

McGonagall awaiting
the wrist-fattening sentence.

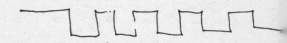

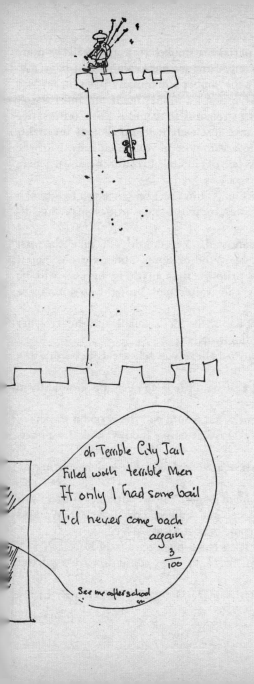

oh Terrible City Jail
Filled with terrible men
If only I had some bail
I'd never come back
     again

$\frac{3}{100}$

See me after school

those animals' parts as a smokescreen and really you are trying to arrest me. Now let me explain. You have mistaken me for a bank robber when really I was on my way to have my prescription for money made up, and I wasn't escaping. The fact remains that under this Conservative government I have lost weight so much that my wrists were too thin to accommodate your handcuffs, with the result that they fell off in the direction of down where they now await you.'

Later a judge said, 'Thin eh? I sentence you to attend a Wrist-fattening Restaurant so that justice may take its course.'

The policeman said, 'Yes m'lord I'll take the first course, the Brown Windsor Soup' and went on, 'and I must warn the prisoner that anything he says will be taken down by the waiter and brought to him on a plate.'

The police bike with McGonagall on the crossbar arrived outside the Dorchester.

'I have reason to believe you sell meals here' said the policeman.

'I cannot tell a lie' said the head chef and showed them a table.

'Now Monsieur, what would you like?' said a waiter.

'Do you serve wrist-fattening foods?' said the policeman.

'Yes sir, we serve anybody' said the waiter putting on a false red nose.

'Quick' said the manager, 'put a spotlight on them this will do for the cabaret' and said to Lovelace Watkins 'You'll have to come back next week.'

'I'll go to the Race Relations Board' said Lovelace.

'Good' said the manager, 'they could do with a cabaret there.'

'Waiter, waiter' said McGonagall, 'there's a fly in my soup.'

'Don't worry' said the waiter, 'the spider in the bread roll will get him.'

'Waiter, waiter' said the policeman. 'What's this?'

'It's bean soup' said the waiter.

'Never mind what it's been, what is it now?'

'Waiter, waiter' said McGonagall, 'there's a hair in my soup.'

'Never mind the greyhound on the bread roll will get him.'

'Waiter, waiter' said the policeman, 'there's a bread roll in my greyhound.'

'Oh dear' said the waiter, 'something's gone wrong you'll have to go back to ordering food.'

There was a storm of cheering from the audience. The policeman removed his helmet and said 'Thank you ladies and gentlemen and now for the first time on any stage . . .' he drew his truncheon and brought it down on McGonagall's head. There was a burst of applause.

'You're the hit of the evening' said the manager, 'you can't stop now.'

Several lumps later McGonagall lay groaning in the number one dressing room. As he came to they were pouring him a cup of tea. 'One or two lumps?' said the manager. 'Seven' said McGonagall. 'Where's the policeman?' he said nervously. 'He said he couldn't wait for you' said the manager, 'he's going it alone. He's been topping at the Palladium for a month now, and he's killed four men already. You're lucky you met him before he was a star.'

'How long have I been unconscious?' said McGonagall.

'A month' said the manager. 'For the first two weeks he was dragging you on stage in a sack and nobody knew you were in it. If it hadn't been for your stomach trouble we'd never have found you. But good news – the judge said you were innocent, and could they have the handcuffs back.' The manager then gave him the bill for the meal and the use of the dressing room. It read –

```
              DORCHESTER HOTEL
                   MENU
Hors d'Oeuvres
   One Spider
   One Fly
   One Bread Roll                    £2. 0. 0.
Soup
   One Bean never mind what it's
   been what is it now soup          £1  3. 6.
   One hair soup
   One greyhound
   One bread roll                    £4. 2. 9.
Entree
   One bread roll in
   greyhound                         £8. 11. 3.
   plus VAT                          £107. 0. 0.
                                    ─────────────
                                     £6,432. 9. 11.
```

The strains of 'I'm a Yankee Doodle Dandy' came floating in under the door through a crack in the ceiling. 'Listen they're playing my music, I'm on' said McGonagall, and so saying he was on, and so saying he was also off and the manager never saw him again.

'Those blows on the head must have done me a power of good' said McGonagall.

CHAPTER XI

India: Jewel of the East

In those days India was a far off land, in these days India is a far off land. The only difference is that in those days it was much earlier. And this applies to McGonagall who is a was rather than was an is. Any questions?

The Eleventh Hussars were the pride of the north west frontier but they were not to know that. But McGonagall knew that and wished to dedicate a poem to their bravery in subduing the tribesmen, tribeswomen, tribeschildren, tribesdogs, tribescats and tribeschickens. 'I must take the caravan route to Isfahan' he said to himself. 'I'm sorry' said the ticket office 'there is no 6.25 camel train leaving Charing Cross today, and my advice to you is to take the train to Dover, then the steam packet to Boulogne.'

'Then what?' asked McGonagall.

'Then I don't give a damn' said the ticket office.

'And you say that no camel trains ever leave from Charing Cross?' asked McGonagall.

'Not to my knowledge' said the ticket salesman, 'but then I'm only on during the day.'

'Oh dear' said McGonagall, 'I need to get onto the caravan route to Isfahan.'

'Well I won't stop you' said the ticket salesman. 'There's a very nice caravan site near Dagenham.'

'Is that anywhere near Isfahan?' asked McGonagall.

'Yes I should imagine it is anywhere near Isfahan' said the ticket salesman.

It was a puzzled caravan dweller at Dagenham who was awakened from his bed at three in the morning in the middle of a thunderstorm by a Scottish voice crying,

'Can you put me right for the caravan route for Isfahan?'

'Farnham?' said the caravan dweller, 'Yes, you see that rain?'

'Aye' said McGonagall.

'Well follow that.'

Meticulously McGonagall followed the instructions and the rain finally led him to Dover where he caught a packet. The Packet cost him a packet because halfway across he was robbed by a fellow passenger, himself without the fare. 'None but the brave deserve the fare.' The fact that the thief was a red Indian has no bearing on the story whatsoever, but at a Sioux Camp in the Black Hills of Nevada an Indian Chief was heard to say, 'We're one short.' He was in fact the sole survivor of the Wounded Knee Massacre and was pretty short himself, five foot two in fact. Which brings us to McGonagall who was short himself having just been robbed. 'Aye, if ah'd only been at Wounded Knee ma'sel' we might have won.' At which time the Captain of the ship was saying –

'What's a nice Red Indian survivor of Wounded Knee doing with Napoleon's Crown Jewels?'

'Me want white man ticket.

> Me go Paris in the Springtime
> Me go Paris in the Fall
> Me go Paris in the Winter when it drizzles
> Me go Paris in the Summer when it sizzles
> Me go Paris every moment
> Every moment me apart
> Me love Paris?

Why oh why do me love Paris?
Because it six thousand miles from
    Wounded Knee Battle.'

'Yes, your papers appear to be in order' said the captain, locking the piano with the Indian inside it. 'He'll never know the difference' said the captain, donning the Napoleonic Crown.

'Good morning Emperor Napoleon' said McGonagall as the captain stepped onto the deck. 'I suppose ye're gae'n hame at last?'

'Oh yes Oui Oui' said the captain, 'I'm going back to mon palace at Fontainbleu, the grub's very good there mon ami.'

'Is that anywhere near the caravan route for Isfahan?'

'Yes, it's anywhere near the caravan route for Isfahan.'

'It's nice of you to be frank with me' said McGonagall.

'Yes I'll be Frank with you, but I will be Tom and Dick with anybody else.'

'What's that noise?' said McGonagall.

'It's a Red Indian playing a ship's piano from the inside' said the Emperor Napoleon.

'They get everywhere' said McGonagall. 'Have you tried Rentokil?'

'Yes' said the Captain, 'they said it was a Red Indian playing a piano from the inside, and there was no cure.'

'You mean? ...' said McGonagall, leaning forward on one foot and clenching and unclenching his fists ...

'Yes' said the Captain, 'the piano will die of Red Indian' ... 'Bit by bit. Bit by bit it will turn to a fine powdery dust.'

Putting on a false red nose McGonagall unclenched his fists and said,

'I've been waiting years to crack this joke – so the Red Indian will bite the dust.'

'No' said the Captain, 'before I slammed the lid on

McGONAGALL TRYING
TO CRACK RED INDIAN
JOKE WHILE
REHEARSING
SWORD DANCE

him, I dropped in a vacuum cleaner so that I could cheat you of that joke.'

A Red Indian stepped onto the deck holding up a vacuum-cleaner dust-bag. 'Your piano I think' he said. 'No, it's the wrong shape' said the Emperor Napoleon. 'Just a minute' McGonagall said, 'set your teeth into that dustbag.' The Indian complied, but did not bite the dust-bag. 'I'll never get this joke across' said McGonagall but rather than waste the occasion, asked 'Chief are you any-where near the caravan trail Isfahan?' 'No' said the In-dian, 'but I have uncle who live near caravan trail Is-fahan. He mighty chief. He great warrior. He have many scalps round waist.'

'What is he doing in Isfahan?' said McGonagall.

'He work for great Shah.'

'What as?'

'He rat catcher.'

'You said he was a great warrior with scalps round his waist' said McGonagall pulling his hat tighter round his head.

'Yes rat-scalps – he rodent operator.'

'He operates on rodents?' said McGonagall.

'Yes him got to eat' said Indian. So saying he handed McGonagall a letter of introduction. The way to Isfahan was open.

'This ship's going awfa' slae can ye no go any quicker?'

'Yes I can' said Captain the Emperor Napoleon Bona-parte, and dived over the side and swam rapidly away from the ship to prove his point.

Seizing his opportunity McGonagall diverted the ship to Persia.

'My God, hasn't Boulogne changed' said the Chief En-gineer as they passed Aden, 'I suppose the captain knows what he's doing.'

Which was true, he was in bed drinking champagne

with Mlle Fifi le Bon bon, known to members of the Merchant Service as Miss Whiplash, strict disciplinarian as the great welts on their persons proved.

But none of them were near the great caravan trail to Isfahan which left the way clear for McGonagall.

'Bloodthirsty pirates!' shouted an honest sailor, pointing to a dhow full of innocent tourists.

Then 'Bloodthirsty tourists!' shouted McGonagall, pointing to dhow full of innocent pirates.

The warnings worked out well. The bloodthirsty tourists attacked the honest sailors. The honest sailors attacked the innocent pirates. The pirates attacked the empty bloodthirsty tourist boat. The innocent pirates then attacked the bloodthirsty tourists, leaving the honest sailors in the innocent pirates' vessel. An honest moment the Royal Navy intervened and attacked the honest sailors in the innocent pirates' vessel. An honest sailor hurriedly sent a semaphore message 'Don't shoot we are honest sailors.' 'Too late' came the reply, 'it's on its way.' At which moment a 16in shell went through the bottom of the boat.

McGonagall hailed the Royal Naval vessel, 'Ahoy there' he said and a lot of good it did him. There was nought for him to do but swim. 'Help' said McGonagall reading from a textbook, 'I cannae swim!' 'Then bloody well drown!' shouted an honest sailor. 'That's something else I can't do' said McGonagall, 'for God's sake drop me a line.' 'Right, what's your address?' replied the voice of his new found pen-friend. 'It's in my other jacket.' 'Very well' said the pen-friend, 'I'll write to your other jacket.'

McGonagall spent a troubled month at sea clinging to an assortment of upturned objects.

> One inverted moustache cup
> One coil of yarn rope
> One wicker dog's cradle

One inverted porcelain soup basin
One inverted commas
One tin of Glaxo
One empty Cider Bottle
One reserve coffin
One gill prawns in plastic bag
One dust-bag containing a fine powdered
   piano and one Red Indian jockstrap
   made of rat scalps
One squollich
One Thog
One Toryallglyt.

There are many other items still unrecovered and we leave space here for the reader to list these as and when the information arises.

**Readers listing space
for arising information
As and When.**

↓

How was he to know that the mighty tidal currents would ease him across the mighty Indian Ocean, up the mighty Indus to the foreshore adjacent to the barracks of the 11th Hussars who were busy watering their horses.

To the simple mind of Gunga Din who was watering his feet, the sight of a Scottish bard rising draggletailed from his watery bower caused him to say, 'God save me and my water.'

'Ooooooooooooh' said the figure. At this sound, as one, the horses fled in terror.

'Ooooooooooh' it came again.

'It must be foggy tonight on the river' said Colonel Waterballs, 'the fog horns are going full blast.'

'Oooooooooooooohhh' it went on for several hours.

'Ooooooooooooooooooh, sod it' he said finally admitting defeat.

'The muse has forsaken me – take me to your leader' he said to Gunga Din.

'No' said Gunga Din 'you take me to yours – you look better off.'

'Do not muck about dark laddie – my wrists and I are starving to death – what have ye got tae eat?'

'Water' said Gunga Din.

'Anything else?' said McGonagall.

'There's only me' said Din.

'Right then take me to your water' said McGonagall.

'You're standing in it.'

'That's not good enough' said McGonagall, 'I'm used to mixing with people like Captain the Emperor Napoleon Bonaparte of the Channel Packet, now *there's* water for you.'

'Oh yes sir I can see, like Queen Victoria, you're a man of breeding, I can see them breeding from here.'

That night McGonagall slept in a dung hut. 'It may not look much to you Mr Machonochie' said Gunga Din, 'but to a dung beetle it is home.'

Oooooooooooh wonderful comfortable hoose of
    dung,
For too long your praises have been left unsung,
But this night to be in it has been a great treat,
And has kept me dry from my head to my feet.
What more can I say about this humble abode?
But to build one this big, a cow has to do
    quite a load.

This poem moved Gunga Din greatly, in fact it moved
him to throw a bucket of reeking Hindu slops over him.
'I ordered water' said McGonagall. 'I know' said Din,
'but it's the best I could do at this time of night – water
is very short just now.'

'Very well' said McGonagall, 'fetch me a short water
and a chota peg.'

Gunga Din fetched a chota peg which McGonagall immediately drove into the ground with a chota mallet and
hung his hat on it. 'Ah that's better' he said, 'I can see
the Himalayas, I wonder if they can see me.'

The place was strangely empty, no sound broke the
silent air. No tread of martial troops about which he
had often read in the Boys Own Paper.

'Where are all Queen Victoria's Redcoats' said Mc-
Gonagall.

'They're at the cleaners' said Din. 'Remember the
dinner Queen Victoria threw?'

'Aye' said McGonagall.

'It struck the 3rd Battalion Grenadier Guards who
were on their way to India to stop the British Troops killing the natives – mainly the 11th Hussars. At this moment
sahib' said Gunga Din 'the Hussars are at Fort Night'.

'Fort Night?' said McGonagall, 'that must be all of two
weeks' march away.'

'Saddle me a horse' said McGonagall.

'I'm sorry sahib this is a foot regiment' said Din.

'Then saddle me a foot' said McGonagall and so saying he hit himself with a stick and galloped away on one leg. 'I can't let down the 11th Hussars' said McGonagall. 'Why not?' said Gunga Din, 'everybody else has.'

'I must write a poem about their achievements.'

'They haven't got any' said Gunga Din.

'Then what can I write about?' said McGonagall.

'Right about turn' barked Gunga Din. Which sent McGonagall bounding in the opposite direction, head on into the ranks of the 2nd Battalion Tundapandi Chokdhas, (4th Battalion Coldstream Guards who turned out to be the Skinners 2nd Light Horse – the first one having died of a heart attack the week before.)

'Who in God's name are you?' roared Captain Skinner, drawing his sword.

'You cannae fool me with that drawing' said McGonagall. 'It's not even a good likeness.'

'Nonsense, it's a very good likeness, but a very bad drawing of a sword,' said Skinner.

'I am racing to the aid of the 11th Hussars' said McGonagall, still bounding around on one leg.

'So it's true, they're short of one-legged men?' said Skinner.

'No' said McGonagall, 'they're short of two-legged poets.'

'But you only have one leg' said Skinner uncorking a bottle of Cockburn.

McGonagall smiled and raised his kilt revealing the other. He then raised the other and revealed his leg.

'My God, you're a fine figure of a man (about $9\frac{3}{4}$, I should say) we could get all the washing on that on a good drying day. Take a swig of this' he said passing the port.

'Thank you' said McGonagall raising the port and lowering his kilt.

'Is this Cockburns?' he said.

'Yes' said Skinner.

'I've got quite a few of my own' said McGonagall.

'We've no time to lose' said Skinner, withdrawing the port. 'Cheers' he added, filled up his boot, and drank it.

'I've plenty of time to lose' said McGonagall snatching the boot and draining it to the toe.

'I still insist' said Skinner, filling up his other boot, 'we have no time to waste. Every minute is precious' he said as he emptied a second bottle.

'I'll drink to that' said McGonagall, 'as I have more time,' and he took a third bottle from Skinner's saddle-bag from which he proceeded to take great knee-crippling drafts.

'You must stop delaying me like this' said Skinner opening yet a fourth bottle.

'I will nae' keep ye lang' said McGonagall, 'but I'll keep ye Cockburns.'

In a flash he inserted a rubber tube into the fourth bottle and drained it to the dregs. 'It's quicker by tube' he gasped.

'Taylor Walkers Fine Old Reserve 1879' said McGonagall.

'Correct' said Skinner, 'except that it's Dow's Fine Old Tawny 1902'.

'My port must be slow' said McGonagall.

'Making a grand total of £39. 8 rupees and 2 roubles as I bank in three different countries. You see my bank has branches everywhere as the head office is in a tree.'

'We've no time to lose' said McGonagall frantically searching for his watch.

'Oh yes you have' said Skinner pocketing it.

'We must hurry sahib' said Gunga Din, 'the 11th Hussars cannot survive for much longer without water, meat and two veg, and rice pudding with a spoonful of jam in the middle.'

So saying the three men took off in hot pursuit. A

lonely figure standing in the mud tower of the besieged Fort Night, his keen eyes searching the road for reinforcements, shouted 'I am a lonely figure in a mud tower of a besicged Fort Night, my keen eyes searching the road for reinforcements and I have just shouted – *I surrender.*'

'You'll get promotion for this' said Captain Flashman who had been waiting all day with his hands in the air. 'I couldn't have held out much longer' he said, 'I was going to have to bring them down for lunch, that's why I'm holding a knife and fork in them.'

The cry of 'I surrender' was taken up by the rest of the regiment who were walking around in great droves with their hands in the air, shouting 'White Flag, White Flag.'

But their plans had misfired. Their dreaded enemy The Red Bladder and his swarming Mad Mullahs were also shouting, 'We Surrender & Company Limited – White Flag, White Flag.' Even in moments like this there was no need to be unbusinesslike.

'Oh no you don't' shouted Flashman, 'we surrendered first.'

'Oh no you didn't' said the Red Bladder and Co. Ltd 'we were first, so take that, sailor.'

'All right' said Flashman, 'I'll take that sailor, but I insist that we surrendered first.'

'Charge' screamed the Red Bladder & Co. Ltd to the faithful Mad Mullahs, 'attack the infidels until they admit that we surrendered first.'

Waving a white sword Flashman & Co. leapt onto the parapet. 'Fight them lads – remember we're fighting to surrender ... Give up as soon as you can ... Don't shoot when you see the whites of their eyes, don't fight to the last man, don't shoot to the last round, and unfix bayonets. If anybody wants me I'm theirs.' All that day both sides spent their time screaming, and running away from each other, but neither side would admit victory. As fast

117

as one side hauled up a white flag the other side hauled it down again.

That night both sides lay exhausted from a hard day's surrendering. McGonagall saw the plight of these two great armies.

'Ooooooooooooooooooh'

> 'Twas on the third of June in the Year of 1883
> When the 11th Hussars (who incidentally are a
>   regiment of Cavalry)
> Went out to fight the dreaded foe amongst the
>   foothills near
> They saw the Red Bladder with a mighty host
>   and they all cried 'Oh dear'
> But brave Captain Flashman on his horse said,
>   'Do not fear my men
> 'As soon as we've surrendered we can all go
>   home again.'
> 'Oh no' the bold Red Bladder said, 'it's our
>   turn to give in.'
> 'If we go on like this' said Flashman, 'no-one's
>   going to win.'
>
> All day long the battle raged with both sides
>   trying to lose.
> Both sides were such terrible cowards there was
>   nothing between them for to choose.
> But true blue British Cowardice finally won the
>   day.
> They farted at Red Bladder and slowly marched
>   away.

The words of the poem died on his lips, to be followed by a great silence, as was usual on most of his public appearances.

All the while Gunga Din was passing among the troops administering a mixture of water, meat & two veg. and rice pudding with jam in the middle, which he poured from a cowskin bladder, and one-time mother to a veal cutlet, that went 'Moo' when a fork was inserted in it. 'This is underdone' said an angered diner, 'I've seen cows hurt worse than this and live.' 'I think you're in the wrong story' said Captain Flashman. 'So I am' said Orson Welles, 'I thought this was Citizen Kane'. 'No that was yesterday' said Flashman, 'today it's Red Bladder versus the 11th Hussars.' 'What's the score?' said Orson Welles. 'Bladder 3, 11th Hussars 11, making a grand total of 22'.

CHAPTER XII

It was a momentous day in the history of the North West frontier of India. For his part in the battle McGonagall was mentioned in dispatches. It went like this –

'McGonagall must be despatched at once'

Next day with the serried ranks drawn up in the square McGonagall received his award from Lord Elphinstone. A Captain read the citation, and from a satin cushion Lord Elphinstone took a Regimental Target and strapped it to McGonagall's head. It was only when the final order 'Take aim' was given that McGonagall realized that all was not well.

'It's goin' to be a braw black moonlacht nacht tonacht' he said, 'but I'm not waiting for it.' Hoisting his kilt he set off at a tremendous gallop on the road to Mandalay, where he had heard the flying fishes play, and the dawn comes up like thunder out of China 'cross the Bay, or mind you it could have been a rumour, because run as he might he saw none of these things.

Every time he passed a military post, a hail of bullets sang around his ears.

It was a lovely song which went like this –

'Around his ears – tum ty tum,
Around his ears tum ty tum'

(The reader can try this on a rifle himself one day.

Take loaded rifle and sing down barrel 'BANG'. It leads to hours of endless fun ending in a Mental Home, or death, both entirely Tax Free, and a worthwhile investment in these hard times. It gives you the choice of dying for your country or your money.)

Of course – the target was still around his head. 'This could be dangerous' he said and posted it to the wraith-like spectre landlord with a message,
'Dear Landlord,

As a token of my esteem for you, will you wear it always in lieu of rent?'

We are coming to what was probably the most momentous something-or-other in McGonagall's life. Lurking in the green glades of Assam are a ferocious tribe called the Shans. They are noted for removing one's head and/or knackers. Now McGonagall unfortunately happened to have both of these artifacts. When he regained consciousness he was in a grass hut with a monkey. 'So they got you too' were McGonagall's first words. At that moment a mountainous woman came into the hut and said, 'I've killed fourteen husbands and you're next.' She threw him on the nuptial and had her way with him.

'Och here Jock, this is real gude' he said to her in a muffled voice from beneath 20 stone of quivering blubber.

'I hope I'm nae hurting ye dear?' he added. 'Two and two are four' he further added, and he was right, she did have four. So this is what must have killed the other fourteen.

It was three non-stop days later when the shagged-out remains of McGonagall weakly said, 'How do you keep this up dear?' And she said, 'it's something that the cook puts in our meat-pies'. 'For your sake, my sake and for God's sake I think I should have one' said McGonagall. She took him to the chef's hut where they were greeted by a small black dog. 'My God' said McGonagall, 'look at the size of that wee doggie's doodle.' 'Yes' said the Queen, 'and he only licks the plates.'

McGonagall devoured forty-two meat-pies, licked the plates, and three days later they buried the Queen. The day after that they buried the dog and the monkey, and the day after that the tribe ran away. 'Come back' shouted McGonagall, 'I was just getting the hang of things.'

The Monsoons came, and they couldn't have come at a worse time bang in the middle of the rainy season. McGonagall himself felt like another bang in the middle of the rainy season. A Colonel stepped out of a tree and fired a pistol into the air which was yet another bang in the middle of the rainy season.

'I'm Colonel Major Dennis Bloodnock, Indian Army Retd.'

'I know' said McGonagall 'I saw them retiring. Why are you living in a tree?'

'So that I can have a bang in the middle of the rainy season. Any more damn fool questions?'

'Allow me to introduce myself' said McGonagall. 'So far I am William T. McGonagall, poet, actor, adventurer and beetroot skinner.'

'Beetroot skinner?' asked Bloodnock.

'Aye a man has tae eat' said McGonagall and ate Colonel Bloodnock.

He continued on his merry way, whistling. 'I'm twice the man I used to be' said McGonagall, 'I wonder what's for supper?' The answer was not long in coming – he was. – A tiger ate him.

It was two days later when an embarrassed McGonagall stepped out of the tiger at a taxidermists. 'I'm so sorry' said the taxidermist, 'I didn't know there was anybody in.'

'You should have knocked' cautioned McGonagall.

'I'm sorry, there was no knocker on this tiger.'

'Then you should have rung' said McGonagall, 'now can I use your phone?'

'We haven't got one' said the taxidermist, 'but we have a flower pot.'

'Well I'll use that then' said McGonagall, and filled it to the brim.

He made a careful note in his diary

> '3rd Sept. 1887 – Did not meet Queen Victoria, Def. Imp. again today, making it six years now to the day. Can she be avoiding me?

At which moment Queen Victoria was writing

> 'It is six years to the day since I first started avoiding McGonagall, and not once has he seen through my disguise which is that of the Queen of England. I notice an improvement in John Brown since he started importing meat pies from Burma, and my own dear Albert too seems much improved since he started licking the plates.'

At which moment Albert was screaming 'Quick, Quick, put the hoses on it!'

By some incredible case of mistaken identity McGonagall was booked to appear at the Pegu Club in Rangoon before the Governor General, Sir Isaac Grocks, and the Hon. Mrs Daisy Skreggs, who both packed the house that night. Alas, on the opening night they didn't show, and he played to capacity emptiness.

'Ooooooooooooooh' his opening groans rang round the empty galleries.

'Hurry up' said the doorkeeper, 'we're waiting to lock up.'

'You go ahead' said McGonagall, and he did. He locked him up.

Had there been an audience they would have been puzzled by his finale which lasted eight hours, and consisted entirely of hammering on the door and shouting, 'For Christ's sake let me out.'

He was let out in the morning by the dawn picket.

'I'm sorry sorr' said Sgt O'Rourke, 'we'll have to take you with us.'

'What's the charge' said McGonagall.

'There is no charge sorr' said the Sergeant, 'it's absolutely free sorr. We've been told that you are to have an audience with the king.'

'Ah' said McGonagall, 'that's where the audience must have been last night – with the king, and quite obviously I was at the wrong place. Lead on O'Rourke.'

AS THE LEANING TOWER OF PISA

'As you wish' said O'Rourke, putting the lead on him and dragging him to the Royal Palace.

King Thibor observed the whole scene through his telescope.

'Watch out lads' he said, 'they're bringing him here. Hide the silver, keep the meat pies locked up, and don't let him lick any of the plates.'

All was calm as McGonagall was dragged through the Dragon Gates. Above him towered the 300 ft gold covered Sule Pagoda. At the top was its diadem of rubies, diamonds, and pearls, and on each side the priceless hand-beaten silver screens.

'A nice place you have here' said McGonagall.

'No it's not' said the Sergeant, 'this is only the chicken house, wait until you see the real thing.'

So McGonagall waited to see King Thibor's real thing.

The Burmese King stood up on a golden stool and raised his arms to Heaven.

'My God I've never seen arms sae long as that' said McGonagall.

'Don't be too impressed' said the Sergeant, 'they're false.'

'Mae minga lllllllllloooooo' chanted the king.
The priests answered, 'Ooooooh Yicki Hacki Doolah'
The hundred wives said, 'Corr.'
'Now bring McGonagall forward' said the king.
'Time' said McGonagall

BOWEL SUFFERERS, WHY SUFFER?

DR RANK ZEROX'S FINE MIST KAOLIN MORPH contains rindled sneck now available in the 800 ton handy family pack complete with free copper bowel pan on stilts for tall members. Additional iodine-impregnated string ready for immediate knotting. Also free silver-plated leg-clamps with iron stirrups given with book of porridge recipes and smooth 12 bore shotgun, with instructions on how to escape.

PLEASE BEWARE OF IMITATIONS

especially   Maurice Chevalier

            James Cagney

and   Humphrey Bogart

'What was that?' said King Thibor.

'A natural break' said McGonagall, 'the woods are full of them.'

'That's funny, I thought they were trees,' said the king.

'I've come a long way' said McGonagall, 'and I have reason to believe that you are waiting to give me an ancient burial order.'

'Aye' said the king, 'Get out.'

'I don't like your tone of voice' said McGonagall.

'Very well' said the king, 'I'll try it higher.'

'Get out' he said, in E flat.

'I will not' said McGonagall in G sharp.

'Now' said the king in the key of C, pulling his right leg up his back, and over his left shoulder, with the instep under his chin and his foot on the blind side.

'Can you do this?'

'Not if I can help it' said McGonagall.

'Well for Christ's sake help me' said the king, 'I can't help it, it's a rare disease only caught by Burmese Kings and then only when standing on one leg.'

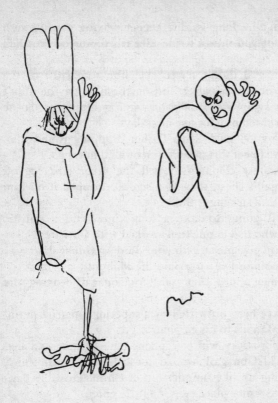

'Don't come near me' said McGonagall, 'I don't want to catch it.'

'Well catch this' said the king, and threw a tree at him.

'What's this?' said McGonagall from underneath.

'It's a natural break' said the king, 'the woods are full of them.'

'It's crushing my chest' said McGonagall.

'It's all part of the ceremony' said the king, 'you are now the holder of the Order of the White Elephant of Burmah (Crushed Chest Division).'

'Where's the white elephant?' said McGonagall.

'It won't be long' said a keeper waving a whitewash brush, 'but you mustn't ride him till tomorrow 'cos he's still wet.'

McGonagall didn't try to ride him tomorrow or the next day or the day after. But on the next day he didn't ride him again, nor finally on the day after that. So he had not ridden him for five next days.

'It's no good' said King Thibor, hopping round him, 'we'll have to get this tree off him or he'll never go.'

Two stately elephants raised the great teak log off McGonagall's chest, then at a signal, dropped it on him again with a sickening thud.

'This is going to take a long time' said a sadistic Mahout who had at one time worked with Christie.

'Can you give me an estimate?' said McGonagall.

'Four pounds ten a ton' said the Mahout.

'I cannae afford that' said McGonagall leaving the shop.

'We have been outwitted by a superior financial brain' said the Mahout to his elephants.

Riding a sticky white elephant (the painter had lied to him) McGonagall headed towards 'the dawn which was coming up like thunder out of China 'cross the bay'. It sounded a nice place even if a little noisy.

'Solly' said a Chinese frontier guard.

'I'm not Solly' said McGonagall, 'you're thinking of Solly Black who died years ago through a shortage of commission.'

'Solly Black' said the guard, 'only White Dlip-dly elephants arrowed in Chinky-Poo Land.'

'But this is The Order of the White Elephant' said McGonagall.

'Me velly solly Black we have not ordered any White Elephants' said the guard, 'but we have ordered the following

        small blown loaf
        $\frac{1}{2}$ pound laspberries
        $\frac{1}{2}$ pound laddishes
        1 bottle losc hip syrup
        1 tin lollmops'

'Tee hee – no flozen flesh apalagus?' said McGonagall.

'No, no frozen fresh asparagus' said the guard, whipping off his mask. It was the French Gendarme with the false red nose. 'Alors got you again' he said, 'it's a long time between jokes but they're worth waiting for.'

'Well I'm not waiting for the next one' said McGonagall and left.

CHAPTER XIII

It was the 9.25 White Elephant for Siberia but McGonagall didn't know this and neither did Siberia. They were both in for a nasty shock. It is completely inexplicable as to why 100 rhesus monkeys in the prime of their life should suddenly fall from a tree onto the back of the passing McGonagall. The fact remains that McGonagall looked over his shoulder and remarked, 'Look, there's a tree suffering from loss of monkeys.' And nobody could be more up to date than that.

These are the hard facts that we have to accept, that there was at that moment a white elephant bearing a hundred monkeys and William McGonagall bound for Siberia. Follow that.

Following that we arrived at a notice which said in Hindu Kusch: 'Kabadar both krab Iskamuffit – 1 mile'. McGonagall was still wrestling with the translation as he, 100 monkeys (late of a tree), and a white elephant sank majestically into a quicksand which fortunately was going slow that day owing to the shortage. 'I've got it' said McGonagall, 'that notice said DANGER – SLOW – QUICKSAND AHEAD and/or DEADLY MORASS – Please tick which is applicable.'

At the mention of the word 'tick' the now off-white elephant (who lived in mortal terror of small insects) screamed a scream. Curling its trunk around McGonagall it pulled itself out leaving him in.

'Come lads' he said to the hundred monkeys, 'those years of tree climbing must have paid dividends.' The lead monkey clicked his heels, saluted smartly, climbed under McGonagall's kilt, and made a small adjustment. There followed a terrible Gaelic scream, and the monkeys watched as McGonagall shot rocket-like from the ooze. 99 monkeys applauded their captain as he too was dragged upwards with McGonagall like a strap-hanger. 'I haven't finished' said the monkey. 'I wish you had' said McGonagall.

Somehow they had cucumber sandwiches for tea. 'I've just remembered' said McGonagall, 'it's my 56th birthday. It's a new experience for me.'

> Oooooooooooh beautiful birthday at the
>   age of 56
> For as a birthday present 100 monkeys did
>   some tricks
> The elephant balanced on a monkey's head
> At the sight of this the other 99 monkeys fled
> Oh 'twas a wonderful sight to see
> As the monkey in turn balanced on a flea

The poem was never finished nor was the trick. You see both the flea and the monkey died, and in that order. The flea's coffin was borne on a mighty gun carriage, and taken to the flea cemetery in Assam where they poked a grave for him. Alas somebody sneezed, and the coffin was never seen again. The grave was filled in by a fleadozer.

FOR SALE – LEAD LIGHT-WEIGHT HOWDAH –

For sale by Maharaja of Yardoo (it's the famous Howdah Yardoo Howdah) complete with useless telephone, and unburied useless flea coffin; also take-away elm tree, piece of knotted string as new, packet of lighter flints which cannot light cigarettes but are much lighter flints than normal. One undriven nail (only one previous owner). One pair Convict's leg-shackles (limbless owner going abroad).

'What was that?' said the off-white elephant.

'That was another commercial break by one of the poorer companies' said McGonagall.

'Halt – who goes there?' barked a voice from out of the stygian night.

'William McGonagall, one elephant, and 99 monkeys as new' replied McGonagall.

'Advance and be recognized' barked the stygian voice.

McGonagall and Company advanced to be recognized.

'I don't recognize you' said the stygian sentry from the crepuscular gloom.

'Well that's your fault' said McGonagall, 'I've been around a long time.'

'Around? – You look more like a square to me' said the crepuscular sentry from the obsidian darkness.

'Where are you?' said McGonagall, at which moment the sun rose and there was nobody there. It was a bitter pill to swallow. McGonagall eased his jockey pants, adjusted his legs, and freed his spats which flew off in the general direction, a wise choice under the circumstances.

'All these years' he said, 'and I never knew they were homing spats.'

At which moment his attention was drawn to the crest of a hill from which emanated sounds of galloping hooves, fried eggs, and the sound of a kettle coming to the boil. The sound picture rang true. The next moment there galloped to the top of the hill a horse, dressed as a chef, with a gas stove on its back on which boiled a kettle adjacent to two frying eggs.

'It's the horse's d'oeuvres' said McGonagall as they sat down to dine.

'This is a fine picture' said an artist called Vincent Van Driver, as he skilfully and furiously painted this unique subject. Years later his completed painting 'Breakfast in a Burmese Clearing' was enough to have him committed to Colney Hatch Asylum, where his picture now hangs – in his cell. As the learned psychiatrist who committed him said, 'Whoever heard of a Scotsman dining with ninety-nine monkeys, an elephant, and a horse dressed as a chef?'

'I have' said McGonagall entering the psychiatrist's padded cell, (which cost extra). 'Oh my God, that's done it' said the psychiatrist, 'now they'll never let me out' as 99 monkeys settled on his head. 'If you can balance on a flea' said the elephant 'I can teach you a great trick that always ends up at the Flea Cemetery in Burma, but for God's sake don't sneeze while you're doing it.'

There was tapping on the wall from the next cell.

'Who's that?' said McGonagall.

'It's Van Driver' came a voice, 'Can I go now?'

'Yes' said the psychiatrist, juggling with monkeys, 'it's my turn to stay.'

Next day Van Driver was back in his cell. Foolishly he had submitted to the Academy, a painting of a psychiatrist juggling with monkeys, entitled 'Paddington Station'. This time the psychiatrists were right. It was a puzzled booking clerk at Paddington who was asked by a traveller for a second class return for the 9.25 monkey-juggling psychiatrist to Leeds.

'You must be joking' said the booking clerk, putting on an Indian headdress, and locking himself in the safe.

'Here's another one' said a male nurse pushing the booking clerk into Van Driver's cell.

'Mother' said Van Driver.

'My son' said the male nurse slamming the door behind him.

'We're a long way from Burma' said Van Driver.

'Well you ought to know' said the male nurse, 'you always had a good eye for distances.'

'Yes, this is the one' said Van Driver pointing to it. He appeared to be playing the lead on this page.

The great bell tower boomed in the great citadel at Moscow. From inside the Tsar's Palace the Royal Romanoff Orchestra, of 120 musicians and one mechanic, played The Great Waltzes from Rimsky Korsakoff's Scheherezade, all of which was wasted on McGonagall who was asleep on a park bench in Finsbury Park, N.12.

'I have a feeling I'm missing something in Moscow' said McGonagall in N.12.

'Hello, hello, hello' said a policeman three times, or three policemen once.

'Move along now, you are breaking bye-law 3, section 7 and one of the legs on that park bench.'

'Och but constibule 'tis the season o' Gude Will, and a Merry Christmas and a Happy New Year to ye.'

'What are you talking about, it's the third of March?'

'Och a merry third of March, and a Happy New fourth of March to ye, and Shude Auld Acquaintance be forgae' he sang.

'Speak English you foreign bastard' said the policeman, raising his truncheon.

'Stay your hand policeman' said a tall stentorian voice that stood 6 ft by inches 3, and wore a black top hat with crepe.

'My card' he said offering it to McGonagall and, 'my fist' he said offering it to the policeman.

The policeman went down passing McGonagall who was on his way up.

McGonagall peered through the gloom at the card. 'It says you're the Ace of Spades' he said.

'No' said the stranger, 'that was my father, he was a coloured World War One Fighter Pilot. He was shot up by the Red Baron, and then shot down by the Blue Max who were both colour blind.'

'I'd say they were colour prejudiced' said McGonagall.

'You've said it,' said the Voice 'but they were too late, by the time he hit the ground he was dead – you see the machine he flew had been grounded.'

'Why, what was it?' said McGonagall.

'A 74 tram' said the voice, 'You see it was foggy when he took off, and he never knew the difference – he only became suspicious when a rear gunner behind him shouted, "Any more fares please?" You should have seen the gas bill they sent him afterwards.'

'What's that got to do with it' said McGonagall.

'Nothing, I merely mentioned that you should have seen the gas bill they sent him.'

'Why did you want *me* to see it?' said McGonagall, jettisoning his newspapers.

'I thought perhaps in this half light you might pay it' said the voice.

'Not on your Nellie' said McGonagall.

'Very well then, pay it but not on my Nellie' said the tall voice.

'I still don't know who you are' said McGonagall.

'Neither do I' said the tall voice, 'we'll have to wait till the fog lifts.'

'Haven't you any idea at all who you are?'

'Yes, Piccadilly Circus.'

'*You're* Piccadilly Circus?' said McGonagall.

'Yes.'

'Good, this is where I get off.'

'No, not yet – wait till the fog lifts' said the tall voice.

The man lowered his tall voice, 'Come' he said, 'you look as if you could do with a ride to my house.'

It turned out that the stranger was none other than a stranger, his name was Professor Frankenstein-Doctor Jekell-Mister Hyde-Count Dracula-Stranger.

McGonagall introduced himself as William T. McGonagall, nee Breakfast in a Burmese Clearing by Van

Driver. 'I see we both have illustrious names' said the professor.

'Yes, and I know an aircraft carrier which has one' said the Breakfast in a Burmese Clearing.

'I'm going to ask my butler to fetch me a bean on toast' said the professor who was also an economist.

'Can you fetch me one?' said McGonagall.

'Certainly sir' said the butler and fetched him one with the tray.

'Quick' said the professor passing him a hand mirror, 'if you look in this mirror you will see on your cheek a perfect replica of our family's coat of arms in reverse.'

'Thank you' he said admiring the imprint.

'Of course this will cost extra' said the voice, still shrouded in its own fog.

'I see the fog never seems to leave you' said Breakfast in a Burmese Clearing nee McGonagall.

'Yes it belonged to my mother' said the tall voice, 'and I'm very attached to it. Would you like to raise your hands above your head now?'

'What for?' said McGonagall.

'For this' said the voice, and a pistol appeared from the fog.

'You can't fool me' said McGonagall, 'that's a water pistol.'

'Yes' said the voice, 'but I happen to know you can't swim. I heard you mention that you were the "Breakfast in a Burmese Clearing" by Vincent Van Driver' said the voice, 'and that is worth all of pounds 2,000,000.'

'You mean ... ?' started McGonagall and paused –

'You mean what?' said the voice.

'You mean bastard' concluded McGonagall, 'and I'm not "Breakfast in a Burmese Clearing", I'm an original William T. McGonagall of Dundee, Poet, Tragedian, Actor and Beetroot Skinner by appointment to Her

Majesty Queen Victoria and Prince "Put the Hoses on Him" Albert.' A jet of water hit McGonagall in the chest. 'You shouldn't have said that' said Prince Albert emerging from the fog. He made a certain gesture from the waist down which hurt.

'Help,' said the bedraggled McGonagall, as the Prince Consort flushed him down the stairs into the coal cellar, up through the manhole, and into the street.

A policeman observed a coal black figure, with one eye drowning, lying in the gutter shouting – 'For one week only – Scottish Gutter Singing.' Under the circumstances this seemed a ridiculous thing to say which would never stand up in a coat of law, which is why he was saying it lying down without a coat on, but he thought it would draw attention to his sorry plight, which was strapped to his right leg with a rubber band which used to be his mother's.

'Pardon me sir, is that your sorry plight?' said the policeman.

'Yes, but a man's a man for a' that' said McGonagall.

'Lend me your helmet constable' he said. The police-

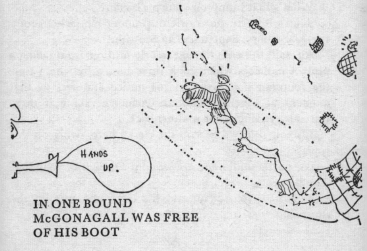

**IN ONE BOUND
McGONAGALL WAS FREE
OF HIS BOOT**

man handed it across and McGonagall filled it to the brim. 'Thank you' he said jumping on the back of a passing page-boy, saying, 'Hurry, take me to the next page I don't like the one I'm on.'

'Thank God for that' said McGonagall, 'that policeman was about to force me to ask him the time, not to mention Thulg.'

'Thulg?' said the page.

'I told you not to mention it' said McGonagall. 'That is a magic Fijian word only to be used during a severe attack of bowel trouble called Thulg.'

'Thulg?' queried the page.

'Oh God,' you've said it again' screamed McGonagall, and with the whites of his eyes showing he ran backwards into the coal cellar shouting, 'Nurse – the screens, the screens.'

'You've been down the coal hole nearly four hours' said the great Treacle Millionaire Lord Elpus to a shattered footman holding an empty coal bucket full of filth. 'You won't believe this milord, but I was struck from above by a Flying Scotsman.'

'What's that hump on your back man?'

'That's him sir, he crawled up under me jacket shouting "Sanctuary, Sanctuary" in Scottish.'

'Ah' said the enlightened treacle millionaire quaffing a pint of molasses which took three hours, by which time the footman had given in his notice and was at that moment at Finchley Labour Exchange asking if there were any vacancies for a hunchback.

'It's your lucky day' said the clerk, 'here, swing on this rope.'

The footman did and crashed out through the window. The bell rang.

'That's all for today' said the clerk and put up the shutters.

At the Quasimodo Hospital for Deformed Hunchbacks, 13 Piles Road, Hackney, the wards rang with the screams of 'Sanctuary, Sanctuary' as scores of humpty backs kept disappearing up to the roof on bell ropes and crashing down again. 'If only we could get some of them into bed' said one worried doctor, 'we might be able to cure 'em.' 'One of 'em has been in here three years and we haven't got his name yet.'

'We can't go on like this' said a very haggard senior surgeon clutching the remains of his Harley Street suit – in this case a vest, one sock and half a plimsoll.

'If we could only catch one we could get his wallet.'

At which moment one of the quasimodos dropped his hump which hit the floor with a sickening cry of 'Ochhhh'. 'At last a cure' cried the surgeon. There was a scream from the now humpless Quasimodo, as without his counterweight he shot up at twice the speed and disappeared up the great bell which came crashing down over McGonagall.

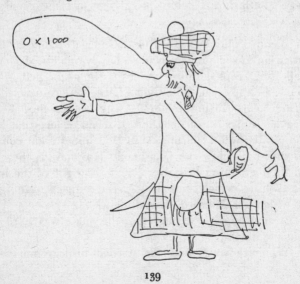

From inside the bell the surgeon heard –

Oooooooooohhhhhhhhhh
OOOOoooooooooooooooohhhhhh
OOOOOooooooooooooh
To end up like this is very sad
Considering the happy times in the past I've
    recently had
I'm just back from Burma, a land of much grace
Where I dined with an elephant and 99
    monkeys at the back of their place.
We were painted whilst eating by an artist of
    renown
And some bits were green and the rest of it was
    brown.
Since doing that painting he has done no other
But he's often been visited by the elephant's
    brother
So you understand why I think this moment is
    hell
Trapped with Quasimodo under this naughty
    bell.

So ends Volume One of the McGonagall Fantasia. The situation at the moment is not a happy one for McGonagall as he keeps shouting under the rim of the bell, 'This is nae a happy situation.' Camel Laird were contracted to bring heavy lifting material, with which they lifted heavier things on top of the bell to make sure that McGonagall couldn't escape. Will that honeymoon couple in that flat below the Quasimodo Hospital, as they lay in their groaning bed, ever forget the sight of the lone Scottish leg, which came through the ceiling at midnight, to which was strapped a sorry plight?

Even stranger, hanging from the ankle was Lord El-pus's footman.

'Who are you?' said the startled bridegroom, withdrawing to a safe distance. 'You'll find this hard to be-lieve' said the footman, 'but this ankle I am clutching is the end of Volume One.'

And so it was.

ANY QUESTIONS?

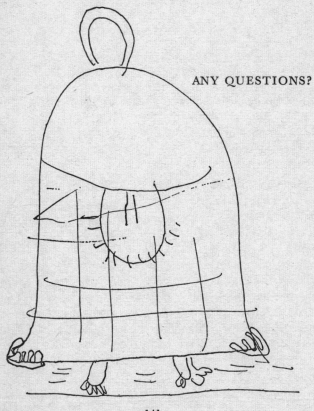

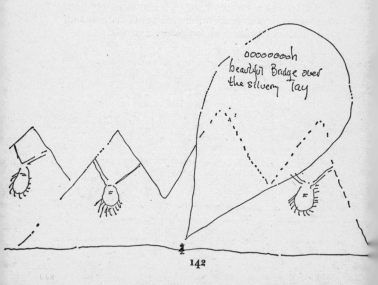

ooooooooh
beautiful Bridge over
the silvery Tay

142

MORE ABOUT PENGUINS
AND PELICANS

Penguinews, which appears every month, contains details of all the new books issued by Penguins as they are published. From time to time it is supplemented by *Penguins in Print*, which is our complete list of almost 5,000 titles.

A specimen copy of *Penguinews* will be sent to you free on request. Please write to Dept EP, Penguin Books Ltd, Harmondsworth, Middlesex, for your copy.

In the U.S.A.: For a complete list of books available from Penguins in the United States write to Dept CS, Penguin Books, 625 Madison Avenue, New York, New York 10022.

In Canada: For a complete list of books available from Penguins in Canada write to Penguin Books Canada Ltd, 2801 John Street, Markham, Ontario L3R 1B4.